Alligator Smiles

A Tale of Romance
&
Hidden Crime
Under the Florida Sun

BY

BLYTHE RAINEY-CUYLER

When Debra Price, an arts executive from California, accepts a job on the Gulf Coast of Florida she finds herself an outsider in the rural, tropical setting and a victim of a conspiracy. Hired to develop a cultural park, she unknowingly upsets a good ol' boy network of drug smuggling and a land scam. The men have secret plans for the park. The more successful Debra is, the more she encounters their resistance which soon escalates into violence. Innocent people are killed, and the tropical serenity of the Gulf Coast explodes into a battle between retirees, land developers, old Floridian families and state politicians. Debra learns that, like the smiles on alligators, charming Southern manners can hide dangerous thoughts. She also learns about love and personal bravery as she takes a stand that risks her life and exposes corruption that reaches Tallahassee, the state capital.

Table of Contents

PART 1

Chapter One

P eople along that particular coastline didn't go out much at night. They had moved to Palmetto County, Florida, for the tropical climate, but something about its primitive nature made them uncomfortable. The sounds of alligators mating in the moonlit canals next to their homes frightened them. The strange pre-dawn cries of unusual birds made them uneasy. The newest inhabitants of what used to be a swamp played bridge at night, or watched television, or went to their development's clubhouse once a week to play bingo.

Highway 19 was almost deserted at night. That's why it was easy for the two men in the black sedan to follow her. They had been watching the office building for four hours before she came out and got into her car. Their instructions were simple: terrorize the woman in the BMW. Get rough if necessary.

She saw the headlights coming up fast from behind, but she assumed the car would just speed past her on the empty highway.

Probably just some kids with a lot of beer under their belts, she thought.

When the car braked at her rear bumper and stayed right on it, she was angry.

"Okay, hotshots. I'm driving at the speed limit. You want to go faster, you go around me," she muttered.

The car stayed at her bumper, nudging it occasionally, for a mile. She refused to go faster. She was a woman not easily intimidated or frightened. People knew her as a tall, strong woman of middle age who was naturally optimistic with an easy laughter, even after the early death of her beloved husband.

Dammit. I'm not going to play this game. She put on her turn signal when she saw an intersection ahead on the right.

Just then the car pulled off her tail as if to pass. Instead of passing her car it moved alongside. When she turned her startled face to look at the car she saw two men — perhaps Cubans, was her impression — in the front seat of a battered black sedan. The dark man on the passenger side grinned at her and mouthed an obscenity that communicated his intent even through closed windows.

She missed the intersection and her chance for escape. Scared, she began to drive faster. She said a frantic prayer aloud, "God! Make them leave me alone, please!"

They kept dangerously close.

She was frightened now and not thinking clearly. She floored the accelerator to eighty miles an hour. Possible escape routes flashed by her. The black sedan stayed abreast, toying with her, nearly scraping the car.

Then they came at her hard, not worried about any damage to their car. Feeling the impact and hearing the grind of metal on metal, she swung the steering wheel sharply to the right. Her last thought as her car flew off the road at over eighty miles an hour was, *This can't be happening!*

An elderly man, getting into his car in front of the all-night pharmacy, saw the BMW hurl toward him. It hit the telephone pole fifty feet from where he stood. The sound of the crash stunned him. He saw the black sedan slow down momentarily and then speed away. It was ten minutes before the help he summoned from the pharmacy's telephone pulled the woman from the burning car. By that time the Cubans were already south, past Port Pompano. They were arguing about which restaurant in Miami served the best black bean soup.

———

Twenty years ago not even that old man would have been there to see the crash. Back then, a few fishermen and their families lived in stilt shacks built over the swamps that extended out into the shallow waters of the Gulf of Mexico. Their small, almost flat boats shared the humid swamp with tropical birds that knew, as the fishermen did, that the wilderness provided food. Until recently, there was nothing of interest here to anyone except those fishermen and birds. Certainly there was nothing worth killing for.

This part of the coast had simply been overlooked when Nature had parceled out environments that could be used to turn a profit. Only fifteen miles south of the county line stretched miles of pure, quartz-filled white sand that sloped gently into the tropical water and provided a lucrative playground all the way down to the Keys.

Twenty miles north of Palmetto County's swampy coastline, warm springs, once treasured by Indians, had been converted into "natural wonders." Thirty years ago middle-class tourists, in family-filled cars, stopped at the springs on their way to the white beaches farther south. They watched "mermaids" swim underwater in spring-fed tanks and surreptitiously sip air from hidden hoses.

Most tourists didn't stop when they drove through the area just south of the springs. The few who did were enticed by hand-printed signs that read "See Man Wrestle Alligator" and "See Wild Animals." In fact, on the exact spot where the woman burned thirty years later, there had been a mangy, caged gorilla haphazardly tended by a man who also handled snakes. For twenty-five cents the tourists could watch snakes entwine the man and the gorilla sleep.

The interior of Palmetto County was as quiet as the coast, but for different reasons. Like the fishermen, the inhabitants had been there a long time and were few in number. However, most of them were wealthy. They owned large citrus groves and cattle ranches begun by early settlers who had seen the advantages of year-round warmth and the vast acres of palmetto-dotted flat land.

A town was established thirty miles inland from the neglected coast, on the site of the last battle between the U.S. Army and the Seminole Indians. With no sense of irony, it was named Harmony.

Then the county started to change. For no apparent reason except that it was there, a few cattle ranchers and citrus growers bought coastal swamp land that was useless for growing oranges or grazing cattle. They then forgot about it. However, their heirs had gone to college and they saw what was happening to the rest of Florida. They put landfill over the swamps and built small stucco tract houses. The coastal fishermen and their stilt houses began to disappear. The gorilla died, and the snake handler and the alligator wrestler moved on. Retirees from "up North" began to appear. The land owners, who were now also developers, knew their market — all those blue-collar workers, now retired, who had driven down the coast after seeing the mermaids.

There were no zoning plans or building regulations. The developers just kept filling the swamps, building homes, and putting in inadequate sewer systems, and the retirees kept coming. They lived along the coast in developments named Aloha Place and Palm Haven, on land that really wasn't land. Man-made canals contained the brackish swamp water that commingled with the Gulf water and became the refuge of displaced alligators. A small town was named New Harbor where there had never been an old harbor.

In 1984 the edges of civilization in Palmetto County were rough. There was tension between the old and the new. The Florida natives, or "Crackers," who lived inland, made jokes about the gray-haired new residents who lived on the coast. They were irritated by the retirees' slow driving habits and their complaints about inadequate Southern service.

The new coastal residents were uncomfortable with their predecessors of the swamp. Elderly men, mowing their lawns, found alligators sunning themselves next to ceramic gnomes. Long-legged herons stalked the tiny lizards that clung to screened windows, upsetting the women who looked up from their bridge games to see wriggling lizard tails dripping from long beaks.

The day before the hired killers hunted down the woman on Highway 19, an alligator ate a poodle that made the mistake of relieving itself too close to a backyard canal.

In August 1984, the conflict between the old and new societies came to a head.

Chapter Two

She was having a nightmare when the doorbell rang. In her dream, she walked across an enclosed courtyard toward heavy wood double doors that led to the jungle outside. It was hot. The courtyard and the buildings of the finca were dusty beige. She was answering a summons. Someone wanted to get inside the courtyard. She wondered why she was afraid, and then she knew. Death waited outside. Slowly she opened the doors to a group of young men. Smiling, they told her that they had come to kill everyone on the finca. The family inside had become too powerful. They were sorry, but it had to be done. Their leader wore an alligator belt and a vest made from alligator skins, and he carried a rifle. She knew she was going to die, and a strange feeling of resignation came over her. Women had died like this for centuries, simply because they were part of a place and time.

Then the leader looked closely at her and said she wouldn't die this time. Because she was a smart and pretty woman, she could live for a while longer. She stood by the doors as they entered the courtyard and she heard the screams and saw the fires begin. The leader rang the chapel bell. She woke with a start. The bell kept ringing. She was sweating and didn't know where she was. Only the dream was real to her. Then she saw the bedside clock. It was 10 p.m., it was her doorbell ringing, and she had been asleep since six o'clock. The nightmare fear turned into another fear. Maybe it was vandals again, she thought. But vandals wouldn't ring the doorbell. She was disoriented and couldn't remember why she had fallen asleep so early. She looked down at her rumpled clothes and realized that she had come home from the office exhausted and had not bothered to undress before falling asleep. The week had been frantic, filled with things to do before the telethon. This evening she had given in to her exhaustion.

The doorbell continued to ring. It wasn't too late for someone to come to her house, but she was afraid. She sat on her bed hoping they would go away. Her clothes were damp with perspiration. She had forgotten to turn the air conditioner down from its daytime setting of 82 degrees.

Her fear increased. There was something ominous and terribly urgent in the continuous ringing. She had to stop the sound.

The house was dark and smelled stuffy as she walked with bare feet from the bedroom to the living room. The tile on the hallway floor felt cool to her feet and she wanted to lie down on it. She knew "something bad" was outside wanting to come in, but she had to stop the ringing.

"Who is it?" she asked in a voice tight with anxiety.

"The Sheriff's Department, ma'am. Will you open the door, please?"

For a small fraction of time she thought that if she didn't open the door the "something bad" wouldn't happen. Then she switched on the porch light and opened the door to two deputy sheriffs.

"Are you Debra Price?" the older, heavier deputy said while showing his badge. As she watched him speak she noted idly that flying bugs, already attracted to the porch light, were set-tling on his shoulders. One briefly crawled across his perspiring forehead.

"Yes," and then to begin what was now inevitable, "What's happened?"

"We'd just about decided no one was home. May we come in, please?" The younger one spoke as he waved insects away from his face.

"Of course. I was asleep. What's happened?" She repeated her unanswered question as she backed into the dark living room and they walked toward her, closing the door behind them. Once the door was shut, only a dim light came through the living room curtains from the porch. As Debra switched on a table lamp she felt suddenly embarrassed by her appearance.

Although their faces were impassive, both men were struck by her beauty. The tousled blonde hair, the slender body, and the strikingly attractive face were familiar to them from the public service announcements that ran on local television. Her disheveled appearance now only made her more appealing.

The three of them stood in the light cast by the small lamp. Her question apparently made the deputies feel awkward. Debra wondered how many times she had to ask what had happened. Then the older deputy spoke.

"Did you lend your car to anyone?"

"Betty Lou. Betty Lou's been in an accident?" Debra moved closer to the older man and reached out to touch his arm. The younger deputy coughed nervously.

"Betty Lou Anderson is your office assistant, is that cor-rect?" the older deputy continued without answering her ques-tion. When Debra nodded, he said, "And you let her drive your car tonight, is that correct?"

Debra nodded again and knew she'd have to explain the sit-uation before they told her anything. "Her car is in the garage.

She wanted to work late at the office. I didn't. So I asked her to drive me home and then take my car back to the office. She was going to pick me up here, at home, tomorrow morning. Is she hurt? What happened?"

"She's badly injured, ma'am," the younger deputy said. "She hit a telephone pole and the car caught fire. We got your name when we checked the car ID in Tallahassee. I know this is a shock, ma'am, but we need to know the names of her relatives."

"She doesn't have any close relatives. She mentioned a step-brother in Atlanta that she barely knows. I have his name on her employment application at the office. Will you drive me to the hospital? We can stop at the office on the way." Debra was starting to shake. The "something bad" was now in her world.

"We'll take you to the hospital," the older deputy said, "but I think you should know that reporters came to the accident scene and they're at the hospital now. They know that the car of the executive director of Palmetto Park was involved in an accident. You're a celebrity around here, you know."

———◆———

The hospital waiting room was painted the usual pea-green color. Overhead fans barely moved the slightly air conditioned atmosphere. Even through the heavy double doors that led to the parking lot, Debra could hear the high-pitched sound of the cicadas. Everyone had warned her about August in Florida. Now she knew why. She had been in the shoddy room for an hour already, sticking to the bench and having difficulty breathing the humid air. She was waiting for someone in authority to tell her Betty Lou's condition.

When she had first arrived, two reporters, one from the local TV station and one from the New Harbor newspaper, had questioned her. The newspaper reporter tried to get her to connect the past vandalism of her car with the fact that Betty Lou had been driving it when the accident occurred.

"How can there be any connection? You're stretching it, Fred. What happened tonight was a tragic accident. Isn't that enough?" Debra had established good media relations as part of her job, but tonight the reporters' familiarity was unwelcome.

"There was a witness, Debra," Dave, the television reporter, stated. "The sheriff won't let us talk to him, I guess he's badly shaken, but the word is out that this old guy saw someone force your car right into that pole. The sheriff told us not to release any information about a possible witness, at least not yet. What do you make of that?"

"I 'make' nothing of it right now. Nothing. I just want to know that Betty Lou is all right. That's all, fellows."

With relief, Debra watched them leave to get their stories into the eleven o'clock news and the morning paper. By now, anyone in Palmetto County who watched the late news on the local station would know that the Palmetto Park project was making news again. She wondered if anyone from the board of directors would come to the hospital . . . probably not. This wasn't the kind of publicity they liked, and Betty Lou wasn't one of them. Maybe Luther would come, though. Betty Lou had worked as his secretary at the ranch before he "donated" her to the project along with the land.

An orderly walked past the waiting room, and Debra stopped him before he could disappear behind a door marked "No Admittance."

"How is Betty Lou, the accident victim?" she asked.

"They're working on her, ma'am," the plump young man replied. "I'm not supposed to say anything, but she's burned real bad, ma'am." He was apologetic as he backed into the swinging doors and left.

She returned to the bench under one of the ceiling fans and noticed that the Styrofoam coffee cup she held was empty. As she got more coffee, she looked at herself in the smeared chrome of the vending machine. The harsh fluorescent lights overhead did grim things to the face reflected back. She thought it odd that she had been in Florida seven months and had only a slight tan. Her eyes reminded Debra of those awful paintings of big-eyed children.

She leaned against the coffee machine as she sipped the barely drinkable coffee and thought about the reporters' comments. She wondered where her car, or what was left of it, was now. Her thoughts were scattered, but she didn't see how her car being vandalized in the past could possibly be related to tonight's accident, as the reporter suggested. But thinking about the vandalism and about Betty Lou's accident reminded her of all the difficulties she had encountered in the last few months. Only three months ago, in Tallahassee, Martha had warned her of possible trouble.

At least the late night phone calls, explaining in obscene detail what was going to happen to her, had ceased a month ago. But then everything at work had seemed to go wrong. There were the seemingly endless board meetings where everyone haggled over the smallest decision concerning the development of the park. The work on the park roads had ground to a halt. She couldn't even get a board decision to remove the piles of excess fill that were created by the preliminary road work. Everyone knew the fill was smothering the tree roots and slowly killing the trees near the Nature Center site, yet the executive committee of the board kept blocking any attempt at actionThere were a few people on the board who were just as frustrated as she was. She had decided to channel the frustration she, and those others, felt by planning the telethon. It was a positive action that might generate more community support. But for the last month she felt as if she had been walking under water, weighted down with pressure and moving in slow motion.

More and more the same question came to her mind: how did she ever end up here? Her motives had been naive and too simple: a change of venue, tropical adventure, and a chance to create something of value. She was thirty-five years old and needed her life to take a new direction. She hadn't realized the culture shock that would result. Living for so long in California, she was accustomed to a different life: producing concerts and television shows; being surrounded by artists, musicians, and actors, and sipping wine on terraces that overlooked the Pacific. Now she drank iced tea at Rotary Club luncheons before giving fund-raising speeches to complacent men and she worried about dying trees.

Suddenly the doors leading to the parking lot banged open. Debra jerked at the sound and spilled coffee onto the floor as Johnny's muscular 220-pound body and six-foot, four-inch frame came barreling into the waiting area. He looked solemn but his handsome face registered joy when he saw her by the coffee machine. His dark hair was slightly messed and he was wearing old jeans, beat-up moccasins and a red plaid cotton shirt that he had obviously buttoned in haste; one shirttail hung three inches lower than the other. He intended to stop when he saw Debra, but the momentum of his arrival carried him toward her. Just before impact he opened his arms and she found herself buried in the woodsy, clean smell of his shirt as what was left of her coffee spilled to the floor.

"I can't breathe!" she gasped.

He released her quickly but kept his huge hands on her shoulders. He crouched slightly so that he could look into her face.

"It was on the news. At first I didn't understand. I thought it was you in that car. How is she?"

"I don't know, Johnny. No one has told me anything except that she's badly burned. This whole thing is so unjust! Why her? She's nice and hard-working. We've been through so much together on the project, and I never told her how I appreciated her! Now I realize she may be the only friend I have in this crazy place."

Debra was crying. Johnny patted her shoulder awkwardly.

"Hey. Hey, now. Why, you have lots of people who care about you! You're just all worn out right now. Stop crying, okay? I'll see if I can find someone to tell us something. Maybe Doc Jenkins is around. You just sit right here." Johnny gave her a final pat on her shoulder and gently pushed her down onto the bench. Then he turned and quickly walked through the doors marked "No Admittance."

Debra was ashamed of her self-pitying outburst. She realized that she hadn't thought about Betty Lou for at least ten minutes. Then she smiled when she noticed that the "No Admittance" doors were still swinging from the force of Johnny's exit. He had certainly been relieved to get away from the tears and do something physical.

She wondered what it was like to have so much strength. The combination of his physical strength and his gentleness was endearing. And his paternal instincts toward her amused her. He was at least a few years younger than she and yet, just now, he had made her feel protected and feminine. No wonder the women around here adored him. Of course his appearance probably caused some of that adoration. He had a boyish face on a powerful body. That amazing body had taken him to the top in the Olympics wrestling competition. Now he was seemingly happy to be back home in Palmetto County and working in his own construction firm. Although he was from an old family, he didn't have the arrogance some of the other males from those families possessed. Yet he had taken it for granted that he could walk through doors marked "No Admittance."

She smiled wryly with the thought that someone should have posted "No Admittance" by the county line sign when she had arrived. Then she would have known seven months ago that she wasn't wanted. She would have flown back home. Debra knew that someone, or several people, didn't want her here. She was used to people liking her, and she found it confusing when they didn't. How could her success with the park project — getting state money for it, recruiting volunteer workers — make some people so angry?

It didn't make sense to Debra. She knew that several men on the board of directors were buying land around the park, but so what? They were businessmen who knew the value of the land would increase when the park was developed.

Debra stared at the floor, relieved to have her thoughts drift away from the hospital and the awful waiting. When the short, squat man with the gray crew cut tapped her on her shoulder, she was startled. As always, she recoiled slightly when she saw him. His homely face showed the effects of past fights. A scar ran down one side of his face, his nose had been smashed into a pulp, and his thick glasses distorted his eyes. Debra hoped that he wasn't aware of her reaction. Joe Casey, president of the local chapter of the National Organization of Retired Citizens and board member on the Palmetto Park project, was a retired union organizer from the New Jersey docks. His battered body attested to years of confrontational behavior. Since his retirement he had been verbally confronting Palmetto County commissioners, real estate developers, hospitals, insurance companies, doctors, and anyone else he felt ignored or took advantage of "his people," the working class retirees. He was coarse, loud, and infinitely compassionate. He and Debra had been struggling to communicate across class barriers for months. They had been surprised to find that they liked each other.

"How you doing, kid?" His gruff voice hid his genuine concern.

"Hi, Joe. I'm waiting and worrying. I don't know what's happened to Betty Lou." Debra indicated a place next to her on the bench. "Thanks for coming. Sit down. Did you see it on the news, too?"

"Yeah." Joe sat down but looked ready to jump up at any moment. "Whadda you mean, 'too'? The sheriff's office told me they went to your house with the news and brought you here. Somebody else show up?"

"Johnny's here. He went to find someone who could tell us about her." Debra tried to smooth her disheveled hair, but her hands were shaking.

"Don't worry about her, kid. She's history, I hear. Worry about yourself. "

"You can't mean that," Debra replied.

"I sure as hell do mean it. This wasn't no accident. It was a New Jersey kind of accident. You follow?"

"Oh, Joe. Don't, please," Debra said.

"Come on. Admit it. You were sitting here starting to wonder about things when I walked in, right? The reporters told you about a man seeing a black sedan, didn't they?" He was leaning toward her. Anyone walking in on them would assume he was angry with her.

"How did you find out about the witness? It wasn't on the news, was it?" Debra asked.

"Nope. But I got my sources." Joe was always talking about his "sources" and his "contacts."

"Some old man, who probably shouldn't be on the road himself because of his bad vision, says he saw a car force my car off the road. Really, now! Just because of some vandalism, just because I received some threatening phone calls, just because things are suddenly difficult with the project, you're telling me someone wants to hurt me?"

"And you 'just' listen to yourself, kid," Joe answered.

Johnny walked into the waiting room. He looked pale through his deep tan.

"Glad you're here, Joe. It's bad, Debra," he said.

Debra stood up and put her hand into his.

"They're going to fly her to a burn unit in the morning," Johnny continued. "Right now, Jenkins is working on her trying to stabilize her. He's even called in a specialist from Tampa. He'll be here soon. Debra, I think it was supposed to be you in there and the thought is making me sick."

"Stop it. I don't want to hear what the two of you are implying. No more talk, okay? Let's just get through this with Betty Lou." Her premonition of "something bad" was beginning to overwhelm her with its magnitude. She knew it would be easy for her to give in to her fears.

"You're not going to get off so easy," Joe said. "Johnny and I have had suspicions for a couple of months now. Hell, this ain't no goddamn fairy tale, and, to tell you the truth, I'm goddamn sick of pussyfooting around your tender feelings."

"That's enough, Joe," Johnny said. "Maybe she's right. Maybe it's not the right time. Let's just give it a rest."

Johnny put his arm around Debra as he spoke. They were standing together when Stanley Zaluski, a former county attorney now in private practice and president of the Palmetto Park project, and Alistair Lake, an Australian soccer player who was also the coach of a well-known professional soccer team in Tampa, walked through the outer doors that led to the parking lot.

Both men looked surprised to see Johnny holding Debra. She was embarrassed, but not because of the picture she and Johnny presented. She was embarrassed because not once during the last terrible hours had she thought about Alistair. Not once. And they had been lovers for three months now. As always, Alistair's presence eclipsed everyone else's. His thick blond hair was tousled to perfection and his blue eyes were brilliant in his handsome, tan face. His tall, powerful body carried his expensive navy sports jacket, crisp white shirt, and designer jeans elegantly and he moved with that special grace the very best athletes possess. Debra had never seen him on a soccer field, and she found it difficult to reconcile his elegance with the stories of his sometimes vicious behavior while playing.

The two new arrivals presented visual opposites. Stanley Zaluski was a balding, sallow-faced man of forty-five who looked ten years older. His pear-shaped body was forty pounds overweight, and no matter how expensive his clothes were, they always appeared poorly cut and wrinkled.

"Debra! Thank God it wasn't you! As soon as I heard it on the news I drove up." Johnny moved away from Debra and watched as Alistair embraced her. He had heard that they were dating, but no one in the county had ever seen them together.

"I was just driving in as Alistair arrived. Sorry I couldn't get here sooner. How is she?" Stanley directed his question to Joe Casey, who was still sitting on the bench, watching everyone. Joe barely glanced at Stanley and gave a dismissive shrug of his shoulders in reply. Johnny answered, "Not good, Stanley. Doc Jenkins is working hard to keep her going until she can be transferred to a burn unit."

For the first time since his arrival, Stanley looked at Debra. He moved closer to where she was standing with Alistair.

"This isn't good for the project, Debra. I heard that Betty Lou had a drinking problem. You were foolish to let her borrow your car. She probably had a few too many drinks after leaving the office and lost control. I'll do what I can to keep any negative information from getting out to the public. Meanwhile, as president of the board, I suggest you cancel the telethon and go away for a rest. Just for a while."

Debra's face became even whiter under the harsh lighting. She slowly shook her head and said, "I can't believe you're saying these things. How dare you say she had a drinking problem! You know better than that. Can you see Betty Lou going to a bar alone?"

Stanley dismissed her reaction with a wave of his hand. "Now don't go all dramatic on me," he replied. "Who knows what lonely women do? Luther called me when he heard the news and he sends his deepest regrets that this happened. He said to tell you he's been worried that Betty Lou was working too hard. Apparently, there was some sort of drinking incident when she worked for him. Anyway, he's been feeling that you've both been working too hard and lost perspective on the whole project. He feels maybe you've been going too fast with it. After all, it is his 'baby,' and he always envisioned it being built by community effort, not this high-powered fund-raising stuff. Maybe what's happened, although it's tragic, is just what you needed to pull back some, get a perspective on things. That's what Luther thinks."

"Perspective! Betty Lou may be dying and you're talking about 'perspective'! If Luther has some ideas about how things should be done, he should talk to me directly at an appropriate time!"

Debra's words were carefully spaced for emphasis. The only evidence of her anger was the whiteness of her fingers as she clenched Alistair's arm.

"You're overwrought. You'll understand what I'm talking about when you calm down." Stanley looked at Johnny, hoping he would support his patronizing attitude, but Johnny turned to put some coins into the coffee vending machine.

Joe stood up and walked over to the lawyer, Debra, and Alistair.

"Well, Mister Attorney, that's some speech. Took you over an hour to figure out your attack, didn't it?" Joe said with disgust. "You guys are something else." Turning to look up at Alistair, he continued, "So the news was on a Tampa station, was it? That's real surprising. Guess Palmetto County is starting to rate. What station, Superstar?"

"What? Who are you, anyway? What are you talking about? I just thank God I had the car radio on." Alistair turned his back to the little man and led Debra away toward the parking lot doors. They heard her protest quietly that she had to remain at the hospital. Alistair said "no," then he and Debra turned to look at the group as she spoke.

"Maybe Alistair's right. I'm going home for a few hours. Johnny, I'll be back here in the morning when they transfer her. You go home, too, okay? I'll call you. Joe, thanks for coming. I have to believe everything is going to be all right, okay?" She didn't even look at Stanley.

Joe answered, "Sure, kid." Johnny just nodded and looked solemn.

———◆———

Stanley Zaluski was a troubled man. Anyone who saw his face as he drove away from the hospital would have pitied him. He was burping and vile-tasting bile kept coming up into his throat. One hand on the wheel, he searched frantically with the other to find the chewable antacid tablets somewhere on the front seat.

Goddamn Marcie. Why the hell does she insist we live in St. Pete? By the time I get home I have to turn around and drive back to the goddamn office. He was desperately trying to think of other things — personal things like his stomach and Marcie — to block out his anxiety about what had happened that night.

Oh, shit. I think I'm having an attack or something. Oh, shit, he thought.

Debra's face was haunting him, and Betty Lou's. It was drizzling and each time the windshield wipers swept over the window he saw one of their faces staring at him from the clear area.

How could it come to this? How did he get in so deep? Sure, he had cut a few corners in his practice. But nothing like this. It had just been a few payoffs before, a few extra dollars earned on the side, to pay for Marcie's lifestyle, and his, if he was honest about it. It was easy for a county attorney in an area undergoing development to help the "right" people. People such as real estate developers who wanted the county commissioners to look the other way when environmentally unsound development plans were reviewed. He had "helped" certain people, been paid by them, and now had a private practice with those people as clients. The arrangement had worked well — until now.

When had the easygoing games of the good ol' boys become frightening? Was it at the turkey shoot in January? He remembered how pleased he was to be invited. Now he wondered if that day was the start of his slide down into this dark place.

PART 2

Chapter Three

Even in January, the warm Gulf waters usually protected the coastline from winter frost, but that night the TV weatherman had said to take precautions. The retirees, before going to sleep, wrapped their rosebushes in burlap, just in case. The roses and the people along the coast were snug and warm.

It was a different scene twenty miles inland. Severe frost settled on the tropical vegetation. All night long smudge pots burned in the smaller citrus groves. The wealthy citrus growers, the only ones who could afford the newer method, had high-powered sprinklers spewing water that formed a protective coating of ice on the tree limbs and their precious fruit. The growers didn't see the incongruous beauty of ice shimmering on tropical plants. Another bad frost like the one last month could ruin them.

The county roads that ran west and east inland through large tracts of land were deserted that night. Those who were awake at four a.m. were busy protecting their crops. No one saw the three cars drive along the winding entrance road to Harvey Brown's Georgian home near the college.

The men arrived still sleepy, yet with that expectant feeling that preceded a hunt. They settled into high-backed chairs in the game room while Freddie, the beautiful black houseboy, served them chicory coffee laced with brandy. None of the men sitting by the warm fireplace could imagine the community college without its president, Harvey Brown. His power within Palmetto County, his gracious home adjoining the main campus near Harmony, and his penchant for using attractive college students as household help were part of the folklore of the area.

Feeling fortified and warmer, the group, which now included Harvey, left the house and drove in the pre-dawn cold to Luther's land. They parked their cars along the county road and walked single file on a footpath through the darkness. They stopped when they came to a strand of scrub pines that encircled a small clearing. Luther's ranch house was five miles south through tangled brush and palmettos. He let them use his land for hunting, Bobby had explained to Stanley, but he never joined the hunt. He didn't like to be involved in killing.

Bobby Schneider had organized this hunt, a wild turkey shoot. He had talked with Luther first and they had agreed on whom to invite. Two of the chosen three often went wild hog hunting with Bobby and all of them sat on the board of directors of the Palmetto Park project.

Stanley Zaluski was pleased to finally be included in a hunt. Bobby had called him two days ago and had carefully explained the procedure to him. However, Stanley was pretty sure he'd make a fool of himself. After all these years, he still saw himself as a poor fat boy from Chicago who knew how to read books but not how to play sports.

Thank God we won't be shooting wild pigs, thought Stanley, as he stumbled into the clearing. He had gone pheasant hunting with his father-in-law once, and he reasoned that a turkey shoot would be similar. As he understood it, they would go to several areas known to be frequented by mating turkeys. In each area the men would wait, hidden, until Bobby blew a mating call on his hen whistle. One or more male turkeys would appear and go into a mating dance. Then someone would shoot the turkey. Protocol gave Bobby the first shot, since he had arranged the hunt.

The rules seemed straightforward, and Stanley was comfortable with them. What he wasn't comfortable about was walking in the dark through the heavy tropical growth. He kept reassuring himself that snakes and alligators slept when it was cold.

The men stood uncertainly in the small moonlit clearing until Bobby positioned them in a line behind some thick bushes. Stanley squatted behind his designated bush and felt ridiculous. He couldn't see the other men but he could hear them as they took their positions.

There was something in the scrub pine next to him. He could hear movement. As he looked up, pine needles fell on his forehead. Then Bobby's soft Southern voice drifted down.

"Hope you fellows are comfortable on that hard, cold ground. I've found me the perfect roost. I figure if you're hunting a turkey it helps to think like one."

Bobby often amazed Stanley. He was equally at ease in a boardroom or sitting in a tree with a rifle across his lap. Stanley felt a swift pang of envy. Bobby was everything he wasn't. He was slim, handsome, athletic, ten years younger, and wealthy.

Stanley shifted his awkward, bulky body and wondered if the other two men on the ground were also wishing they had the ability to scale a tree so nonchalantly. They were an odd assortment of hunters. Ever since Bobby's phone call inviting him, Stanley had been aware that this wasn't just a turkey shoot. The men had been selected for a reason.

Harvey Brown, now there was a strange fellow, thought Stanley. He was an ex-Army officer with a master's degree in education who, upon returning to the county from Korea, had found the small community college the perfect base from which to use his command skills. Through political intrigue, expert fund-raising, and good ol' boy contacts, he had helped the college expand into two campuses, one near Harmony and one in the middle of the county on land Luther had donated.

Harvey made Stanley uneasy. His stiff posture and stern white face contrasted oddly with his fleshy lips and his high-pitched laugh. Although he was outwardly congenial, there was a coolness about him that made him appear cadaverous.

Stanley could hear Rufus Ullman wheezing somewhere to his right. He sounded just like his name, thought Stanley, just like an old dog. A skinny, stooped man of seventy, he wore his few strands of faded blond hair carefully combed across his bald head. He was the trust officer of the largest bank in Palmetto County and had kept the position for thirty years. Stanley often wondered why Rufus didn't have his crooked brown teeth fixed.

How could he fancy himself a ladies' man with those teeth? Apparently, he didn't know that the widows he courted and the dying old women he patted on the hand detested him. Stanley had heard him say, more than once, "Have to keep those old gals happy. How do you think I keep expanding the trust department?" They probably turned their money over to the bank just to get Rufus to stop his "courting," Stanley mused.

The men gathered in the clearing that morning appeared dissimilar but they had two things in common. They were all powerful men in the county, Stanley included, and they had been hand-picked by Luther to sit on the board of his non-profit organization. Stanley decided that whatever was going to be discussed on this hunt had to do with the Palmetto Park project. He wondered when Bobby was going to use the hen call. The silence was oppressive.

"Shit. My balls have turned to ice." Rufus's hoarse voice made Stanley jump. "You fellows don't mind if I rub them to get them warm, do you?"

"Just as long as you don't ask us to help," Harvey replied quietly.

"It won't be long now," Bobby said from his perch. "At first light I'll start the calling. You all positioned safely?"

"Hell, yes, boy," Rufus answered. "We're all hunkered down here in a row. Why, Harvey here is really getting into it. He's starting to look like a hen in heat. Those poor deceived bastards aren't going to know what hit them. You've got first shot, boy, but after that watch out."

Stanley snickered at Rufus's humor and moved his borrowed rifle into a more comfortable position.

Then Bobby blew the hen call. It was a plaintive sound that filled the clearing. The first hint of daylight appeared and it seemed to Stanley that the call had summoned the dawn. Glancing up, he saw Bobby sitting on a tree limb looking like a woodland Pan.

Bobby continued the beckoning call as the sky lightened and the black dense foliage assumed its green color. Just as Stanley was thinking that it was unfair to use the sexual urge to lure and kill, a slight rustling sound caught his attention. A large wild turkey walked into the clearing. Assuming center stage, it flapped its wings and began to stomp its feet in a strange and beautiful dance, accompanied by the sound of the hen call. The rising sun reflected on the bird's opened wings that swooped and dipped in graceful movements. Its black feathers were highlighted by brilliant iridescent colors.

The dance was the epitome of male pride and arrogance. Forevermore Stanley would know the meaning of the phrase "to strut one's stuff." He had never experienced within himself even a glimmer of that male gonadal pride. He was entranced by the spectacle.

The hen call ceased. Then a shot rang out that caused Stanley to jerk and let out an involuntary gasp. The turkey, too, jerked off the ground, gave a startled cry, and collapsed in an undignified position.

All the men except Stanley rushed into the clearing to examine the bird and exclaim over its size. Harvey and Rufus complimented Bobby on his clean shot.

Three more times that morning the scene was repeated. Bobby took the men to different areas, positioned them, used the hen call, and gave each man a chance to kill a dancing turkey. Stanley was last and handled himself well, to the other men's private surprise. They didn't know that he was numb with cold and disgust. By his shot, the last of the day, he had observed a pathetic phenomenon. The dead turkeys had lost their iridescent colors. Their arrogant beauty faded with death.

As the men walked from the last site back to their cars, each carrying a turkey slung over his shoulder, Bobby began the discussion that Stanley had anticipated.

"It's time the search committee made a preliminary selection. Since we advertised for an executive director we've had forty responses. And all of us, including Luther and Jim, who couldn't be here today, have read each one. Luther thinks it's time to fly in the two top contenders for interviews."

"Hell, Bobby, why are you even bothering to ask us? Which two does Luther want us to talk to?" Rufus asked.

"The woman from Atlanta and the woman from California," Bobby replied.

Harvey said, "That's crazy," and gave his high-pitched laugh that always set Stanley's teeth on edge.

Rufus snorted disdainfully and said, "You serious, boy? Now, don't get me wrong, both these ladies sound real fine, that's for sure. Graduate degrees and accomplishments up the wazoo. But they're women, and not only that, they're women who've never lived in the country and who wouldn't know how to supervise putting in a septic tank or grading a road if their lives depended upon it."

Stanley was thinking quickly. What Rufus said was true; those two women didn't have the type of experience the project needed at this stage. When Bobby had been president of the board six months ago, he and Luther had written the job descriptions. They must have had a reason to list what they did.

"If you remember, Rufus, the job description emphasizes the need for a background in performing arts and prior supervision of cultural events," Stanley stated. "There was no reference to land development expertise."

"Let me get this straight," Harvey interjected. "We want someone from outside who can give the project some prestige, whether or not they have a background to deal with land development, is that correct?"

"You hit on it, Harvey," Bobby replied.

Stanley began to understand Luther's real reasons, and felt compelled to be more candid. "At this time, we want the project to continue as a nonprofit organization. We need more credibility within the community. People are beginning to ask us when we'll do something with the land. By October fifteenth if certain developments don't occur on the land, the three hundred acres Luther donated — and let's be frank; he did it for tax purposes — will revert to the Department of Agriculture. They'll probably put the land up for public auction. That's my understanding of the situation after reading the deed. Luther and the selection committee, that's us, want to show the community that the Palmetto Park project is a sincere effort to provide a cultural park in the county which will enhance our residents' quality of life." Stanley was breathing heavily in his effort to talk while maneuvering through the underbrush.

"It takes you a long time, but I really like the way you phrase things, Counselor," Bobby laughed. "Making you the new president of the board was damned smart of us."

"Maybe I'm a little dense this morning," Harvey said slowly as the men finally reached their cars. He, Rufus, and Stanley were breathing hard from the long walk back. "But if we want the park developed within a certain timeline, and we want the community to support its development, why are we considering some arty type who'll just lend prestige? My God, Bobby, she'll take one walk through that jungle of Luther's, see that we're years away from a performing arts center, and leave."

Rufus was wheezing as he threw his turkey into the trunk. He turned to look at Harvey. "We don't need her to stay for-ever, man. Whichever one we choose will be real dedicated and challenged and organize a few benefits. Now I understand the old man's thinking. Shit, either of those two ladies would be real fine. As long as I'm on the selecting committee, I'm for whichever one is prettiest."

"It's agreed then. As chairman of the committee, I'll arrange the interviews." Bobby spoke as he removed his swamp boots and put on his hand-tooled cowboy boots. He was very particular about keeping his Jaguar clean.

The men were jovial in their leave-taking. Stanley was relieved to be in his comfortable car again. Three thoughts, though, tainted his pleasure in being part of the morning's camaraderie: he kept seeing the contrasting images of the turkeys alive and then dead; he wondered what to do with the dead bird in his trunk, since he had no idea how to prepare it and no desire to eat it, and he was aware that he had just agreed to another good ol' boy conspiracy without knowing the whole agenda. For an instant he had a premonition that something bad would be the outcome of this particular plan. Then he dismissed his concern as exaggerated and concentrated on the problem of what to do with the turkey.

❀ ❀ ❀

Chapter Four

"Florida? There's nothing happening there! You'd be crazy to leave L.A. You're joking, right?" The soundman stopped fiddling with the on-again, off-again microphone and laughed at the woman standing next to him on the stage.

"It's just a job <u>interview</u>, Frank. They're probably flying in several applicants. I'd even forgotten that I responded to the notice in the arts journal. Anyway, they called me this morning. Guess I just wanted to try out the idea on you."

Without giving him a chance to continue the conversation, she quickly added, "Do you have a back-up for this piece of junk? If so, get it. We're in count-down here."

He looked startled by her curt tone and left the stage to get another mike from his van. Debra turned to look out into the auditorium while her thoughts ran on two tracks, professional and personal. The professional thoughts were automatic after years of producing concerts: the audience was arriving too early; the volunteer ushers were nowhere in sight, and a ten-spot light was out. Her personal thoughts were not as orderly or predictable. She wondered why she was behaving so bitchy lately. Producing four school concerts a week was probably taking its toil on her. And then there was the absence of Dirk. She quickly concentrated on tonight's program again. This concert would be different from the others. She had convinced UCLA to donate their performing arts hall for a benefit to aid two good causes — their performing arts scholarship fund and the "Arts-in-the-Schools" nonprofit organization of which she was executive director. Alumni of the performing arts department were donating their talents tonight and she had programmed a good mix of classical and contemporary for both the dance and music portions.

But she couldn't keep her mind on the concert. Just last night, while flipping through television channels, she had suddenly seen Dirk's face and his white-toothed, dimpled smile as he enacted a love scene. It was a movie from four years ago, about the time they had become a not-so-secret couple. It was bizarre to watch all his love-making moves that she knew so well. God! She missed the feel of him. No wonder she was bitchy. For two months she had been without their romantic coupling.

And she had done it to herself. After the affair had gone into its fourth year she took the advice of "well-meaning friends" and gave Dirk an ultimatum: she loved him, she wanted to make plans for their future, and, if he didn't get a divorce, their relationship was ended. She had told him, "Get your divorce proceedings started as you promised me after your separation. Decide if you want us to be together or leave me alone." He left and she was alone. Soon after the ultimatum he left for Canada to star in his new film. Prior to the ultimatum she had coached him in his lines, helped him to keep to his strict pre-film diet, and had planned which weekends she could join him in Montreal. Now she was lonely in Los Angeles without him, bored with her job, and was struggling through waves of low self-esteem. For four years she had fooled herself into believing that she could beat the statistics; the "other woman" would win over the unloved wife, and he and she would build an exciting, creative life together. It was embarrassing to think her love life read like past articles in *Cosmopolitan.*

"Debra! Come talk some sense into David. He's determined to do 'Opus Ten' in its entirety. I reminded him that he agreed to your suggestion to cut it by five minutes and now the jerk won't talk to me. Jeez! Why is it something always happens at the last minute to foul up things?"

Debra's short, pudgy assistant hurried to her from the wings in his usual panic-stricken state. While she calmed him, the soundman passed them with the replacement mike. She gave him a quick smile as a peace offering and then went to talk to "the jerk."

Business as usual, Debra thought, and turned all her energies into making the concert a success. Tonight, after the show, she would think about how to change her life. Maybe they would offer her the job in Florida. Maybe that was the answer.

The Bombay Racquet Club in Beverly Hills was just about to stop serving when the group arrived at ten p.m. after the concert. The maitre d' was gracious even though their arrival meant that he couldn't meet his boyfriend for another hour or so. Restaurant personnel tended to be effusive wherever the group went. The four of them presented a glamorous picture; they were perfectly groomed in the latest fashions and their conversation sparkled with witty remarks and allusions to the latest gossip. No one, seeing them, would have suspected that each of the four had struggled for years to succeed in "the arts." The two men and two women, friends with no romantic involvement, lived on hope, optimism, charm, and the sure knowledge that someday they would be rewarded for their attractiveness and talent. If they had fears they held them to themselves or shared them with their pet cats at four a.m. on the day the rent was due.

Debra didn't have a pet to talk to. She had a loving mother and father in Grosse Pointe, Michigan, who still believed their brilliant ("She has a master's degree in theatre arts!") and beautiful daughter would be happy once she settled down with the right man and, given her wonderful abilities, the right job. She knew they worried about her so far away in seductive Los Angeles.

But Debra had her friends. Christine was a stunningly beautiful, tall, red-haired actress who lived on residuals from past roles in soaps that had gone into syndication. She was nurturing to her friends and taught them her hard-earned survival skills, such as where to buy designer clothes at a discount minus the famous labels. Bryan was distinguished with his salt-and-pepper hair and was a writer of film and television scripts. Once one was bought by a major studio but never produced. His close friends knew he met the rent by writing greeting cards and industrial manuals, but his enthusiasm never lagged — there was always some "big deal" about to happen. Jon was a dapper and witty British composer and pianist who had been living in the States for twenty years. Fifteen years ago he had scored three profitable films in a row and now he lived on the royalties from those hit themes. Nothing profitable had come his way since then. Sometimes he organized jazz festivals and took a percentage of the net. He also played the piano in a few of the most up-scale watering holes in Beverly Hills and Bel Air.

Over the last five years, after seeing one another at the same parties, and responding to some undefined feeling of familiarity, they gradually began to meet at least once a month. An informal support group evolved. The other three considered Debra the most stable of the group because she was involved in the arts yet received a monthly paycheck. Debra felt she was the cowardly one of the group. She believed she lacked the courage to attempt the uncertainty of an acting career. Instead she chose to use her education and administrative ability in the somewhat more secure nonprofit arts arena. In moments when she was being kind to herself she realized that she enjoyed helping people and doing "something worthwhile." However, she also knew that it was easier for her to sell an altruistic idea than to sell herself.

She let them settle into the British colonial ambiance of the dining room after they had all ordered white wine and salads and she listened to their compliments about the concert before telling them about the phone call. Christine was the first to react.

"But, darling, you can't be seriously considering a move to Florida! I can understand taking advantage of a free trip for the interview, but I can't imagine that you'd seriously consider the job if it's offered. I've been to Miami — remember that furrier from New York? — I hated it! People may laugh about the lack of culture in Los Angeles, but it's <u>Florence</u> compared with Miami!"

"The cultural center they're planning is on the west coast of Florida, not the east coast. They have three hundred donated acres to turn into a cultural center and park. <u>I</u> imagine unspoiled beaches and jasmine-laden breezes and white homes with large verandas," Debra replied.

"From what I hear the breezes more often smell of cooking 'crack,'" Bryan laconically added.

"Do you know anyone in the arts education field in Florida?" Jon asked. When Debra shook her head to indicate that she didn't, he continued, "There must be someone who could check out this nonprofit organization for you. Maybe it's all hot air. Listen, I've accepted gigs out-of-town and have wished I hadn't." He was obviously skeptical.

Debra realized that not one of the group thought the job was a "fun idea" (as they named ideas of which they approved), nor did they give any credence to a nonprofit organization in Florida trying to bring cultural experiences to its less famous west coast.

Taking her cue from Christine's comments, Debra smiled and replied, "Hey, guys, I'm just going on an interview, not moving there! They're going to pay the airfare to fly me across country, set me down in some romantically tropical setting, and ask me some questions. And I'll ask them some questions and then I'll leave. I'll bring back plastic flamingoes for all of you."

The rest of the dinner conversation hummed merrily along its usual channels. There was talk about the recent game of musical chairs among the studios' executives, comments about the latest celebrity to check into the Betty Ford Center, Bryan's current deal being negotiated, Christine's recent audition, and, briefly in swift sympathy, there was a reference to Debra having done the "right thing" about Dirk. Debra relaxed into the predictability of the evening while, at the same time, she thought about the trip next week. She wouldn't mention it to the group again. A faint air of hostility had tinged their comments. Perhaps, she thought, they had put so much time and energy into succeeding in Los Angeles that when someone even considered leaving the place it was as if their efforts were invalid. What if a better life existed elsewhere? If so, then they had all been duped by glamorous illusions. Debra was determined that she wouldn't be caught in that trap again; four years with Dirk had taught her a lesson.

Chapter Five

The van had left any sign of civilization forty-five minutes ago. The road it now traveled was dark, only occasionally lit by flashes of light as the van passed solitary roadside establishments with signs stating, "Lounge, Package Liquor." The driver told Debra that he was taking a "shortcut" to New Harbor.

She had the sensation of moving through a dark tunnel. The roadside vegetation was thick and tree branches overhung the two-lane county road. Debra was unaccustomed to flat, dark roads and didn't know what "package liquor lounges" were. The Tampa airport had a semblance of familiarity, although she was amazed at its comparative quiet after the Los Angeles International Airport. She was struck also by the lack of different ethnic groups within the airport terminal. Apparently everyone on the west coast of Florida was white, middle class and over fifty.

Bobby Schneider of the Palmetto Park project had made the travel arrangements for her. He told her to take an "airport limo" to the Holiday Inn in New Harbor. She was the only person requesting transportation to Palmetto County and, consequently, found herself alone with a talkative, inquisitive driver in a small van racing through a dark land.

The driver was her introduction to the soft Southern drawl. It was almost unintelligible to her. Bobby had also had it, but his businesslike manner over the phone had made his comments precise. The driver was relaxed and meandering in his conversation; without a specific context within which to attach meaning, Debra was unable to understand much of what he said.

There were no palm-lined boulevards to announce their arrival into New Harbor. No moonlit Gulf waters reflected the van's headlights. They drove past a dark orange grove, made a right turn, and were suddenly on a wide highway lined with one-storied fast food restaurants, used car lots, and grocery stores. These were not the landscaped shopping malls that Debra knew in California, these were garishly lit, hastily built strip stores, their backs to the dark jungle, their fronts eager to attract passing motorists.

The driver deposited her and her suitcase in the Holiday Inn lobby, doffed his baseball cap, spoke a few mysterious words in farewell, and left her. The lobby, of course, was familiar. What wasn't familiar was the total absence of people, either hired help or customers, at eight o'clock on a Tuesday evening. The air, even inside the lobby, felt damp to Debra, and, although the air-conditioned temperature was similar to Los Angeles' in February, she shivered. There were large watermarks on the inn's carpet and a musty odor pervaded the place. A hand-printed sign was propped next to a metal bell telling potential customers to ring for service. She tapped the top with her index finger and waited.

A plump, rather pretty young woman dressed in tight slacks and a shiny polyester blouse emerged from the door behind the lobby counter.

The blouse had stains under her armpits, which Debra saw when the woman raised her hands to smooth her dark hair. The woman's pleasant face was lively with curiosity, but her movements were languid.

"Good evening, ma'am. Can I help you?"

"Good evening! I'm Debra Price and the Palmetto Park project has reserved a room for me."

"Oh, yeah. Bobby said you'd be here. Here's an envelope — it's sealed — from him, and here's your key. Just go out this side door, up the stairs to the second floor, and keep walking 'til you get to number 210."

"Thank you." Debra took the key and the envelope, picked up her suitcase, and walked to the side door.

"Aren't you going to read what's inside?" the woman asked.

Startled by the question, Debra turned to look at her. The young woman was smiling and watching Debra expectantly. What a strange place, Debra thought. She couldn't imagine such a question coming from a desk clerk in any other part of the States.

"I thought I'd read it in my room," Debra replied with a smile.

The woman giggled and, to Debra's surprise, blushed.

"Oh, Lordy. If that darlin' boy had left me a note I'd be all a-tremble. He's so darned pretty. Why, every girl in the county has her eye on his sweet little ass."

Debra's eyes widened at the unadorned sexuality coming from the woman and then began to laugh. The clerk looked at Debra in surprise and then began to laugh, also. It seemed funnier and funnier to Debra. Gasping for breath, she tore open the envelope and read aloud:

"Dear Ms. Price, Welcome to Palmetto County. Either I or Rufus Ullman will pick you up at 8:30 a.m. for your interview at Stanley Zaluski's office. Sincerely, Bobby Schneider,"

"Not much to it is there?" the woman said with disappointment. "You're not a real close friend of Bobby's then, are you?"

"No, I've never met him. Thank you for the good laugh! By the way, is the dining room open?"

"Until nine o'clock, ma'am. You'd better hurry, though. Mabel always starts to shut down a little early."

Debra smiled all the way to her room. *So the past president of the Palmetto Park project has a 'sweet little ass,' does he?* she mused. Debra knew that when she met him she would find it difficult to keep her eyes off his backside whenever the opportunity presented itself.

Her room fronted a harbor filled with sailboats. It was actually a large canal that ended at the motel, Debra realized. She couldn't see to its end; she surmised it ended at the Gulf. She also noted that the canal couldn't be very deep since every boat, seen dimly by the exterior lights of the motel, appeared to be relatively small with shallow drafts. There was no activity along the dock areas and the condo buildings that faced the motel from across the canal were dark. Debra knew that the "winter season" was in full swing in Florida and was surprised at the lack of activity on this coastline.

She realized that she was very tired and not hungry enough to face "Mabel" in an empty dining room. The snack she had on the plane would hold her until morning. She called the woman at the front desk and requested a seven o'clock wake-up call. Ruefully, she remembered that in California it was early evening, and knew that she would be awake several hours before the wake-up call.

She wasn't. When the phone rang, she was dreaming of Dirk being smothered in a Canadian avalanche while she frantically tried to dig him out. Half-asleep when she answered the phone, she couldn't remember where she was or why the man with a Southern accent was calling her. Automatically she thanked him when he told her it was seven o'clock. Then she remembered she was in Florida and had an interview that morning.

Dressed in her Calvin Klein pin-striped suit (with the labels missing since it was from one of Christine's recommended discount stores), she found her way to the dining room by following the din of conversation and clattering plates. The room was filled with men in short-sleeved shirts eating huge amounts of food and yelling jovially at a harried, but smiling, older woman who managed to respond to their banter while serving them platters of greasy sausages, pancakes, eggs, slabs of ham, and bowls filled with mounds of some white substance. Debra saw a vacant table and walked toward it amid a suddenly hushed atmosphere. She and the waitress were the only women in the room.

As soon as she sat down, the waitress came over. "What'll you have, honey?" she asked.

"A poached egg on wheat toast and a small orange juice, please."

"That's it? No wonder you're thin. You're going to need more than that to face old Rufus and that lawyer, Stanley. I'll bring you a side of grits, too."

Debra looked at the broad retreating back of the waitress, dumbfounded. *Toto, somehow I don't think this is Beverly Hills,* she thought.

Almost every man in the place was staring at her and smiling. She nodded at them and smiled and wished that she had bought a newspaper in the lobby to hide behind. *What do they think I'm going to do? Magic tricks?* she wondered. When she opened her purse, took out her "Day-at-a-Glance," and began to flip through its pages in order to appear busy, the audience turned back to their plates.

Debra surmised that they were local businessmen; they seemed to know each other, and breakfast here was apparently part of their daily ritual. As far as she could tell, there were no travelers except for her.

When her breakfast arrived, Debra had her first experience with grits. She didn't like them. However, under the watchful eyes of the waitress and the male diners, she ate a little of everything, grits included.

By eight-thirty she was in the lobby awaiting either Bobby or Rufus. There was no doubt in her mind which of the two arrived for her when she saw the silver Jaguar sedan pull up to the lobby doors and a blond, well-built but small man get out. Even without seeing him from behind, Debra knew it was Bobby. No one named Rufus would walk with that swagger in fancy beige leather cowboy boots, wearing a Texas-style beige silk suit.

———————

The men were waiting for her in the conference room of Stanley Zaluski's law office, sitting around a long table. They stood when she entered with Bobby and introduced themselves. Her first impression was of countrified charm, and, with the exception of Bobby, general unattractiveness. The five men, named Rufus, Stanley, Luther, Harvey and Jim, exuded the same cheery curiosity and friendliness as the other Floridians she had met since her plane landed — except for the one named Jim Fixx, who barely looked at her. He was a small man with red hair, close-set eyes, and a sharp nose that made him appear fox-like. She had never seen so much gold jewelry on a man except once, on an entertainer in Las Vegas.

The rest of the men presented the very picture of the lauded "Southern hospitality." She was particularly charmed by the oldest of the group, Luther, when he bent his long, thin frame over her hand and kissed it. When he spoke, however, Debra experienced a quick twinge of foreboding.

"Bobby, my boy, you should have sent a messenger ahead to prepare us for this vision of loveliness."

Sweet, <u>but</u> . . . she was accustomed to being treated as an equal in business. Whatever male chauvinism existed in Los Angeles, and there was plenty, was behind one's back, not up front. She wondered which man would be the first to call her "honey" or "little lady."

"Well, little lady, how was your flight?" Rufus, the skinny man with bad teeth asked.

Smiling, she assured the gathering that the flight was fine, the motel comfortable, and that she was eager to learn about their organization.

"That's why we arranged this little get-together — to find out more about each other," the lawyer, Stanley, responded.

The questions were standard for an interview until the pale, tall man named Harvey asked, "Won't your beauty interfere with your ability to supervise the road construction?"

Debra was momentarily nonplussed for two reasons: if she said "no," she was, nevertheless, accepting his appraisal of her looks and, also, it was the first time road construction was mentioned as part of the job. Before she could answer, the odd-looking Jim Fixx, who until now had been silent, spoke.

"Now, Harvey, she doesn't have to worry about wearing a hard hat. Tell us some more about the concerts and benefits you produced, Debra."

The rest of the interview concerned her experience with the performing arts, which the men viewed as important for the projected cultural center. Debra asked when they thought the cultural center would be built. Several of the men answered simultaneously, "As soon as possible." Then Bobby added,

"A few things have to be done on the site first, however. We have created a site plan which shows how the land can best be used." He unfurled a paper tube lying on the table as he spoke.

"Phase One of the plan entails opening the park for nature hikes and picnics and Phase Two involves building the cultural center."

"Do you have the money in place already for Phase One?" Debra asked, and before waiting for an answer, added, "Also, will the executive director just be responsible for Phase Two?"

The men looked at Luther, who cleared his throat and then spoke, "The executive director's primary goal is raising money from the community for the cultural center, but, since Phase One has to be completed first, the executive director will probably have to help raise money for some picnic tables, a few roads, and so forth."

Debra noted two things: they hadn't answered her question regarding money already received, and the idea of road construction was again part of the discussion.

Stanley shuffled a few papers while Luther spoke and then looked briefly at him before addressing Debra.

"The reason we've decided to place some picnic tables, and maybe even a nature center, on the site before concentrating solely on the cultural center is that when the land was donated by Luther, in his late uncle's name, to the organization, a certain minor restriction was placed in the deed. It stipulates that construction of a building must begin on the site prior to October fifteenth of this year or the land goes to the State Department of Agriculture. Well, obviously, we can't begin construction on the cultural center by then, so we'll get the community to donate money for the roads and maybe a nature center and I'll simply tell the state that such site work constitutes construction. Nothing to worry about, really."

Luther started talking over Stanley's last comments. Smiling at Debra, he said, "Our Stanley's quite a lawyer, always wrapped up in legal matters. I'm sure you're more interested in the fund-raising aspect of this position. Well, we're not Los Angeles; we don't have 'society' people supporting the 'arts.' But we have money here. Quite a lot, as a matter of fact. The salary for the executive director, for instance, was donated by friends of this board with a three-year guarantee and yearly renegotiation. And there's money inland in those orange groves and on the cattle ranches. It's also on the coast with the developers. Whoever we hire will get those donations flowing. And that person is going to receive one percent of all funds raised plus salary and benefits, including severance pay, even if the person decides to leave. It'll be a generous contract. Of course, all moving expenses will be paid."

Debra was surprised at the arrangement. If, since graduate school, she had one percent of all the funds raised by her efforts on behalf of nonprofit arts organizations, she'd be quite "comfortable" by now.

Bobby said enthusiastically, "Whoever gets the job can live very well on what we're offering. The cost of living down here is considerably lower than New York or California."

Briefly, Debra wondered about the quality of life "down here." What was there in the county on which to spend money? From what she had seen last night and this morning, there were no gourmet restaurants, chic boutiques, theatres, concert halls, or elegant resorts.

As if sensing her thoughts, Bobby said, "Before your flight out this evening, I'll drive you out to the park site and then show you some nice homes a person can buy for very little money."

The interview was obviously concluded when Luther cleared his throat again and rose from his chair. The other men, and Debra, rose also. After handshakes and "thank you's," she left on her tour with Bobby. It was a fast one. His Jaguar hit eighty miles an hour as soon as they left the town. Debra had swift impressions of thick woods on either side of the county road. Something unpleasant began to impress her also: a large number of dead animals were on the road. The mangled bodies of opossums, raccoons and armadillos were in various stages of decay and caused her to constantly avert her eyes.

"Why doesn't the highway department remove them?" she asked Bobby.

"What? Oh. Those are just 'road kills'. No one has time to waste on them. The vultures do our cleaning up for us."

About ten miles from the coast, Bobby slowed to sixty-five miles an hour and told her they were passing the site of the park. It looked no different from what they had already passed. It was a dense mass of gnarled oaks dripping with moss, scraggly palm trees, large ferns, and squat, bush-like palm trees that Bobby said were "palmettos." A large wood sign facing the road stated, "Future Site of Palmetto Park."

Debra murmured, "Lovely, lovely," in response to Bobby's questions, "What do you think of it? Pretty, isn't it?"

The trip back into town was just as swift, with Bobby jauntily waving to a County Sheriff's patrol car as the Jaguar passed an intersection going eighty miles an hour. When they came to the coast highway and Bobby slowed down somewhat, Debra realized that she hadn't seen the Gulf yet. Stores and fast-food places blocked any view of the water and, since the land was flat, there was no way to see over the commercial buildings.

"I'd love to see the Gulf of Mexico before I leave, and Palmetto County's beaches."

Bobby laughed and said, "I can manage to show you some water, but I can't produce a sandy beach. This whole coastline is one big swamp. The houses I'm going to show you are built on landfills. Even the motel you're staying in is built on fill. That canal outside your room leads to the Gulf. Most of the nice homes around here are on canals. There's a little bit of higher land on the Gulf, but early settlers, like my great-granddaddy, built their homes on it and their heirs aren't about to sell." He turned his face toward hers, which caused her to worry even more about his driving, and continued, "Hey, bet you didn't know that there are lots of shell middens left by the Indians on most of that old property. They're just mounds of dirt now, covering the remains of those early dinners, but some archaeologists are interested in them." Looking ahead again, he said, "Anyway, about those beaches; even our place doesn't have one. We row out through mangroves and swamp to get to where our cruiser is anchored."

The houses Bobby drove past were simple stucco dwellings with tidy lawns. There were palm trees in front of the some of the houses, but most did not have any tropical vegetation, instead the lawns exhibited what seemed to Debra to be Northern plants, such as rose brushes. Bobby explained that there were large screened porches in the back of each house that faced canals. The homes' selling prices sounded ridiculously low to Debra. She knew what waterfront property cost in California. The residential areas were depressingly similar and eerily quiet.

It wasn't until hours later, when she was on the plane going home, that she realized she hadn't bought any campy little plastic flamingos for her friends. She remembered seeing a few large plaster ones on the lawns before the silent houses.

Everyone, except Luther, had been drinking heavily all day. It was a hot sun for early February, they kept saying, and then someone else would say, "Thank God, that cold snap's over." Bobby was passed out on the upper deck of his gently rocking cruiser, and his first tan of the year was going to be a red one. Stanley, Luther, and Jim were still maintaining a semblance of fishing on the stern deck, but their fishing rods were next to them in holders with their lines moving slightly with the gentle roll of the Gulf waters. Luther, wearing a straw cowboy hat, was drinking one beer to the other's four. When Stanley got up from his deck chair to make his way down below to the head, Luther chuckled and said, "Stanley, that's the third trip you've made in the last hour. For a man of your size, you must have one hell of a small bladder."

"It's not only the beer. It's looking at all this water. I've never pissed so much in my life," Stanley responded and continued, weaving slightly, to the stairs. Luther put out his hand to halt his progress.

"It wasn't wise to mention the deed restriction yesterday. You surprised me. I thought you were on the team."

"How can I be on the team, as you say, when nobody tells me what we're playing?" Stanley responded sullenly and brushed past Luther.

"See if you can rouse Bobby while you're up. We need to talk some before heading back," Luther said. "Oh, and bring some iced tea for us, will you? I think we should balance out all the beer."

As soon as Stanley disappeared below, Luther turned to Jim, who was slathering more suntan lotion on his fair skin.

"It's sure nice we have a good fish fry waiting for us at your restaurant, Jim. Lord knows that if we had to depend on our fishing we'd starve. But come to think of it, I do believe we caught us a good one this week, after all."

"What? Oh, yeah, I get it. You mean that gal from California, don't you? Luther, to carry this talk a little further, that one would be a fish-out-of-water down here."

"Precisely. She'll not last six months. Just long enough to give us some credibility in the community and allay suspicions when we do what we plan. She'll leave before she can raise enough money to begin construction on any building. If we're lucky, she'll get us our roads and then take the 'fall' when the project fails. Oh, by the way, I saw the real site development plans. That's good work you and Bobby did."

"Thanks."

"Now listen, only we three own land around there right now and only we know the total plan. Oh, except Rufus. I told him. He says he's happy as hell to think my trust will get bigger. It'll make him look real good at the bank. I wouldn't be surprised if he put some of his own money into the Antilles Development Corporation."

Luther was silent for a moment, musing. Then he said, "No matter what he says, Stanley has a pretty good idea of what's happening. He's put some money with ADC, hasn't he?" When Jim nodded, he continued, "Then he'll know everything soon enough when he learns what the company is doing with his tax shelter money. Old Harvey knows we want the project to fail, but isn't sure why. He probably thinks he might get some of the park land for the college."

They watched Stanley emerge from down below, carrying a pitcher of iced tea and several plastic glasses. He placed everything on a table near Luther and then climbed to the upper deck to rouse Bobby.

Luther said quietly, "It's beyond me how a grown man can be so awkward."

Both Jim and Luther watched with amusement while Stanley shook Bobby's listless body. When Bobby finally responded, they heard an agonized yelp and heard him say, "Jeez! I'm burned! Why the hell didn't you wake me sooner?!"

Luther called to Bobby, "Come down here, boy. I want you to make a phone call to that pretty lady in L.A. as soon as we get to Jim's place." Turning to Jim he added, "I decided to increase the salary. It'll be an offer she can't refuse."

Jim nodded absent-mindedly as he watched a shark cut through the water twenty yards off the starboard side. He wondered what Luther would think if he knew what was happening on the land just north of the park site and what the fishing boats that supplied the "daily catch" at his restaurant carried in their hulls. The old man was naive to think he was in control of this particular scheme. The pretentious fool didn't even know that his own ranch hands were involved.

The shark was a big fellow and was coming in closer. Jim thought it was beautiful.

❊ ❊ ❊

Chapter Six

Everything happened quickly after Bobby's telephone call and her acceptance. She resigned from her job, sold her car, and then watched as movers swept through her apartment and loaded their van for the trip to Florida. Later, she went to a farewell party given by her friends that was more like a wake. She didn't call Dirk about the job. As far as he knew, her ultimatum still stood. She realized that he probably thought he could change her mind, if he thought about it at all during the filming. Her parents, during a lengthy phone conversation, reacted happily to the job change, the salary, and the knowledge she would be closer to them. Debra knew that they were also relieved she was getting away from Dirk, although, diplomatically, he wasn't mentioned. She and her mother had talked about the situation many times, on the phone and during visits. Both her parents had been gracious when meeting him, but it was obvious the relationship worried them.

On her first day in Florida, driving a rental car, she found a small pseudo-Mediterranean house on a canal in New Harbor to rent. Waiting for the moving van to arrive the next day, she stayed at the Holiday Inn the first night. Two days later, leaving a jumble of boxes and furniture in her new home, she scoured Tampa to find the "perfect" used car. There was no question in her mind when she found it — a used red BMW 320I.

On the fourth day in Florida, she took another major step. After drinking a glass of white wine and nursing another one in her hand, she called Dirk in Canada.

"You're going to live there?" he asked. "How can you just leave me like this? Why didn't you ask me first? While you were in L.A. at least we had a chance to work things out. Just remember that it was you who left, who gave up. Not me. I was planning to talk things over with Roberta when I got back in a few months. I loved you. I wanted to plan our life together! Now you've changed everything; you've given up on us."

After she abruptly ended the conversation she realized that he had said "loved," past tense. At first she was angry, but then an overwhelming sadness filled her. She realized that they didn't know each other, not really. There had been four years of late night talks, romantic get-away weekends, wonderful love-making, and, always, discussions about his career, his agent, his manager, and, of course, his problems with his wife and the difficult separation. They had seldom talked about her career or her lack of security both professionally and personally. It was partially her fault because she felt her work was inconsequential next to his, and she never wanted him to know how financially difficult it was to maintain a semblance of the "good life" in West L.A.

"Like hell he was going to talk to Roberta!" she said aloud to the glass of wine still in her hand.

She was composed by the time Stanley arrived to take her to the welcome party planned by the Palmetto Park board of directors. Stanley declined to come in, saying that Marcie, his wife, was waiting in the car and was worried that they would be late. The drive to the restaurant, with Debra in the back seat, was strained. Stanley's wife gave no indication of worry; she simply appeared annoyed at being there at all and she didn't care if Debra knew it. A thin, dark-haired woman, she barely acknowledged Debra except to say, "I can't imagine why someone like you would choose to live here. We live in St. Petersburg. Stanley knows I'd die of boredom if we lived here."

An awkward silence filled the car. With relief, Debra saw that they were turning into the parking lot of the restaurant, a franchised steak house in New Harbor that made a feeble attempt at Tudor architecture.

When they walked into the main dining room, Debra was surprised at the number of people talking in small groups and packed next to the bar. Bobby walked over to her, grinned, and said loudly, "Our new executive director!" He took her hand, raised it over her head and turned her to the crowd.

"Okay, fellows, come see what you bought!"

The din of conversation stopped. A small space cleared around Debra and Bobby, and everyone looked at them. She couldn't believe Bobby was doing this to her. Was this simply boozy good cheer? Or was he intentionally making her feel like a piece of property on an auction block? She forced a smile and tried to pull her hand from Bobby's. She wondered which of the men would be the first to step up to her. Maybe they would inspect her teeth? From the corner of her eye she could see Marcie maliciously smiling.

A short, elderly man with a still powerful body pushed his way through the crowd. He broke Bobby's grasp on Debra's hand and growled at him, "That ain't no way to make a lady welcome."

He then turned to Debra and said, "No part of your salary came from me. I'm not one of these monied boys. I'm just an old retired guy who's glad to greet the 'new kid on the block.' Name's Joe Casey."

He shook her hand vigorously while Bobby said to her, "Joe's on our board, Debra, because, besides being 'an old retired guy,' he heads our largest retiree organization. He's a loyal supporter of the park project."

"Just so long as you do right by my people, boy."

People began to crowd around her and she lost track of the homely old fellow who had, in his unsophisticated way, ended her embarrassment. Most of the men were local businessmen who owned insurance companies, real estate agencies, restaurants and other service industries. The women in the gathering were their wives, except for one or two women realtors. Thirty-six of the businessmen had contributed over a thousand dollars apiece toward her first year's salary and pledged more. Each of them introduced themselves and told her that they saw the park project as a business investment; when it was completed it would attract new residents to the area.

Debra was relieved when dinner was served. Her smile was beginning to feel stiff. Just as she sat down and began to sip the ubiquitous iced tea, Luther walked over to her table gently propelling a frail, elderly woman of tiny proportions. She had snow white hair piled upon her head in an elaborate coiffure and was dressed in a long navy dress with a white lace collar and cuffs. Debra thought she was exquisite, and rose from her chair as the two approached.

"Miss Debra, I'd like you to meet my aunt, Alice Bradenburg. Her husband, my late uncle, founded the Bradenburg ranch and it was Alice's suggestion that I donate some of the land for a park."

"Oh, hush, Luther. I did no such thing. I just went along with your idea. How do you do, my dear? You look just like 'Alice in Wonderland', just like a picture in a child's storybook. Now you must keep your wits about you, you know. Pay no attention to the Mad Hatter."

Before Debra could respond to her, she smiled vaguely at someone, or something, over Debra's shoulder and, leaving Luther's grasp with a gentle tug, she wandered away.

Luther looked apologetically at Debra. "She's a dear, really. But sometimes only she knows what she's talking about. Enjoy your dinner. Oh, wait. Here's our local hero, Johnny. I'd like you to meet him. He's on our board, also."

A handsome, dark haired young man of Atlas-like proportions was trying to negotiate his way between the tables as he concentrated on not spilling the contents of the wine glasses he was carrying in each hand. The earnest look on his boyish face and the way he looked in his business suit, like a gladiator forced to don someone else's clothes, caused Debra to smile.

"Becoming a two-fisted drinker now, Johnny?" Luther asked as the man came nearer to where they stood.

"Me? Oh, no! These are for Mother and Joe." To Debra's amusement, the young man actually blushed. During their introduction he frantically tried to find a place for one of the glasses so that he could shake her hand. Finally, he thrust a glass into Luther's hand, quickly wiped his hand on his suit, and grabbed Debra's in a powerful, painful handshake. She liked him immediately.

After he left them to continue his cautious trek through the crowded room, Debra asked Luther why Johnny was a "hero."

"We're enthusiastic about sports, my dear, and Johnny is the 'local boy' who made it into the Olympics. Captain of the wrestling team."

When Luther left, Debra again began to eat her dinner of steak, potatoes and a vegetable new to her, "greens." Her dinner companions included Rufus, his seventy-something sister, Stanley and Marcie. Bobby's chair was empty. Rufus made a comment to the effect that "the boys at the bar were missing a darn good dinner."

Midway through the heavy dinner and while trying to make conversation with Rufus' listless sister and Stanley's petulant wife (the men were discussing the latest attempt by retirees in a particular subdivision to halt development of a strip mall next to their homes), she felt a hard tap on her shoulder. She smelled liquor-laden breath even before she turned around.

A tall, heavy blond woman with a pretty face stood behind Debra's chair holding a drink in one hand. She wore a very low cut blue dress that displayed her ample breasts, particularly as she bent to bring her head closer to Debra.

"Hi there, honey. Jus' wanted to welcome you to our little ol' community. I'm Martha Weil. Maybe no one has mentioned it to you but dear old Alice and I are the two token females on the board of directors. A drunk and a loony bird." Martha laughed loudly and her drink splashed onto Debra's shoulder.

Debra quickly blotted the spot with her napkin and said, "How nice to meet you, Martha."

"Did I get some drink on you? So sorry. Alice and I are examples of what this climate does to women." Leaning even closer to Debra's upturned face, she hoarsely whispered in her ear, "It's not really the climate, honey, it's the men. Beware of the good ol' boys. They'll do you in every time. Everything is not what it seems."

Rufus, sitting to Debra's left, stopped talking to Stanley. He rose from his chair and put an arm around Martha's waist.

"Now, Martha, you need to get some food. You and Debra can have a nice girl talk another time. Why don't you go find Bobby and tell him his dinner is getting cold?"

The man, Debra noticed, slipped his arm from the woman's waist and placed his hand on her backside. He used his hand to push her away. The woman twisted slightly so that their faces were close to each other's. Debra noticed that the woman didn't seem as drunk as before. Her face was more alert and her body was tensed. Debra also noticed that Stanley and Marcie were intently watching the exchange between the woman and Rufus. A certain hush seemed to have fallen over their table. The blond woman, Martha, loudly stated, "Rufus, you old goat, get your hand off me. And, in case you didn't notice during Bobby's graceful introduction of this woman, he's flying so high he's crossed two county lines already. Now, excuse me, I need to freshen up. My drink, I mean."

Martha left. Debra turned back to the table and kept her eyes on her plate as Rufus sat down. Marcie broke the silence.

"All that money and absolutely no taste at all. What a waste."

Rufus gave a short laugh and said, "Honey-child, I just bet you'd know how to spend it in the right way."

"And right away, too," Stanley added. "No one's a faster spender than my Marcie. Hell, give her three family fortunes in the morning and she'd be at your bank by noon, Rufus, begging for more."

"I've never begged in my life and you know it. And I'm tired of your exaggerations concerning my shopping."

Debra turned to Rufus and said, "From comments tonight, I learned that the nearest concert hall is fifty miles away. Is that correct?"

Rufus looked relieved to bring the conversation back to the project and launched into a sad tale of retirees trying to drive Highway 19 at night in order to see plays and concerts in either St. Petersburg or Tampa and said, "It's dangerous for them. That's why they just sit in their subdivisions, bored. And there's nothing for our young people to do around here, either. We lose all our kids to the big cities as soon as they can leave. The cultural center and park are needed here, and so are you."

Debra thanked him and finished her third glass of iced tea (a waitress kept refilling it from a large pitcher). Her natural optimism wasn't functioning at peak level, and she disliked the idea of finding her way to the ladies' room through the noisy crowd, although with any more iced tea, it was inevitable. She began to replay the disturbing episodes of the evening. She could still get out of her contract, she thought, and head for home. The idea of giving up, even before trying, however, didn't appeal to her. Right then, moving the "greens" around on her plate to fake consumption, she resolved to be open to the different culture and its people; whatever problems lay ahead could be no worse than those she encountered in the past among the "glitterati" of Hollywood, and here she had the chance to do something worthwhile.

Marcie was eager to leave as soon as dinner was over. The proper "goodbyes" and "thank you's" were said, and Debra left with Stanley and Marcie.

The drive home was subdued. At one point Debra thanked Stanley and the directors for arranging "such a nice welcome to Palmetto County" and Marcie laughed.

As they turned into her quiet canal community, Debra noticed that the homes were all dark except for hers. She had left the porch light on and it radiated a soft yellow glow. Stanley didn't offer to see her to the door. Turning to the back seat before she left the car, he said, "Rest up over the weekend. At eight a.m. Monday you'll experience your first board meeting." Their car pulled away even before she reached the porch.

At first she thought a neighbor had left a large orange garden hose coiled on her doorstep. She was aware that her neighbors took their gardening seriously and her lawn did look somewhat parched. Smiling at the not-so-subtle hint, she walked to within four feet of the object at her door. It moved. Debra didn't. A rush of adrenalin hit her and every nerve and muscle was instantly on alert. Her mind controlled the urge to run and clicked into its "snake reference file." This one was fat, long, and resembled certain exotic snakes she had seen at the San Diego Zoo. Its head was almost larger than her hand and its tongue, flicking in and out, was forked. From its size Debra knew its striking distance was more than the four feet that separated them. Remembering jungle adventure films, she very slowly did what was portrayed on the screen; she began to back away from the monster.

Inch by inch, keeping her eyes on the snake, she left the porch. Sweat dripped down her neck and from under her arms down the sides of her dress. Finally, she was on the lawn and away from the pool of light cast over the porch. With a gasp, she turned and ran into the dark street.

Now what? How can I get into my house? she wondered. The surrounding homes were inhabited by slumbering people. What could they do? Maybe they'd give her access to a telephone, she thought; perhaps there was an emergency number to call, an alligator and snake removal squad. There was loose gravel underfoot and, when her shoe scraped some, it gave her an idea. Picking up a handful, she selected the largest piece, took aim, and threw it at the snake. It landed with a sharp sound directly on it. Surprised, Debra remembered that she was always last to be chosen as a softball teammate in grade school because of her lousy pitch. The snake reared its head and began to sway.

Scooping up more gravel, Debra began a pebble bombardment. The snake was definitely irritated. Then, ever so slowly, it unwound itself and slithered off the side of the porch to Debra's right. She watched as it left the reach of the porch light and disappeared into her neighbor's bushes.

Her hands were sweaty as she frantically searched in her purse for the house key. Finding it, and holding the key like a bayonet in front of her, she ran to the door. She was trembling so violently that the key didn't fit into the lock. Debra expected to hear a soft rustling sound to herald the return of the snake.

Finally the key fit and the door opened. Debra was inside in an instant and slammed the door on the horrors of the night. "'Welcome to Palmetto County," she said aloud.

Chapter Seven

I t was just by chance that she happened to glance out of the office window and see him. She had been on the floor stuffing hundreds of copies of a fund-raising letter into envelopes. In one month she had managed to cajole two old desks, two chairs, three battered file cabinets, a used typewriter and two desk lamps from the local business community in New Harbor, but no long table for collating papers or envelope stuffing. Not yet, anyway.

She was tired and stood up to stretch. That's when she saw the Le Baron convertible pull into the parking lot of the office complex and Luther unfold his long, thin body from the car. As he smoothed his ruffled gray hair and reached into the car for his Stetson, Debra frantically tried to find her shoes. She found them in back of the bedraggled potted palm a nice woman had donated.

She looked around the office trying to see it through Luther's eyes. Not bad, really. She had painted all the donated office furniture white and had found framed posters of the New York City Ballet and the Museum of Modern Art for three dollars apiece at K-Mart. The cashier had said to her, "These have been on sale for ages. No one wants words on their pictures," and then had added the free potted palm. Luther would be only the second member of the board to visit the new office of Palmetto Park, Inc. Joe Casey had stopped by last week with mailing lists of all the local associations. She had laughed while reading the name of one: "Cow Belles: The Women's Auxiliary of the Cattlemen's Association."

Often during this first month on the job Debra had felt like a Peace Corps volunteer posted to some remote part of the world. However, she was learning the native customs, and although at the moment she longed to finish her work and go home, she was smiling when Luther came through the door. One custom was to be especially cordial to Luther.

"Good afternoon, pretty lady. You're looking fine and fit. Everybody treating you well?" Luther swept off his hat and bowed over her hand.

"How nice to see you, Mr. Bradenburg. Everything is just fine, thank you. See, the office is coming together." Debra gestured vaguely toward the newly painted furniture.

"Looks like you need a table for the back room, though, so that visitors can walk on the floor. Maybe we have one at the ranch. Remind me when we get there, will you?" Luther asked.

"When we get there?" Debra questioned.

"I figured it's about time you had a tour of my ranch. Since I'm on the board, I'm declaring this office closed. It's Friday afternoon, Miss Executive Director, and you deserve some play time. By the way, where's Betty Lou?"

"I told her to leave early. That old car of hers is overheating. She's at Fred's Garage," Debra replied.

"Well, then, lock up and let's go!" Luther was grinning. He obviously was enjoying his idea of what would be "play time" for her.

Debra groaned inwardly. His idea didn't match hers at all.

"What a nice idea! But I'm not dressed for a walk around the ranch. Maybe I could drive up there tomorrow wearing suitable clothing?" Debra asked.

"We'll use a Jeep. You won't have to set down one little foot," he countered.

And that was that. Debra knew that she had played her only graceful gambit.

Once on the road, Debra decided to relax and enjoy her time with the eccentric old man. She knew he was one of the most powerful men in west central Florida because of his inherited ranch holdings, and she knew that he was responsible for the existence of the organization that paid her. She also quickly learned that he drove like a maniac. Despite his seventy-five years, he charged over the roads ten miles over the speed limit. The top was down, and because of the wind and a Beethoven symphony blaring from the car stereo, they had to shout to be heard.

"I understand that you're making lots of speeches to the Kiwanis and all the other organizations. The word around here is that you're bringing in some sizable contributions already. That right?" Luther boomed in his baritone.

"That's right! The community seems enthusiastic about the project. With the cash contributions and the donated equipment we can start preliminary road work in the park next month!" Debra yelled back.

"That's great. You're really taking the county by storm. Now you be sure to work closely with Bobby and Jim. They have the entire road planning done and it's staked out according to the park design. Bobby's real good at land planning. That's why he's so successful with his residential projects."

Debra nodded rather than trying to yell a response. It was true. Bobby and the other men on the board had done an admirable job deciding how the donated acres should be used.

They had commissioned a land planning company in town to draw a detailed map showing the location of a two thousand-seat performing arts center, hiking trails, and a nature center. She had been to the site, ten miles east of New Harbor, only twice since she'd arrived. Both times Bobby had used his father's four-wheel-drive pickup to drive her through some of the accessible areas, and it had been a new experience for her to climb so high to get to the passenger seat. She hadn't been able to visually superimpose the park design on what she saw as a wild tangle of jungle.

"The future entrance to the park is right there, across the road from my ranch," Luther yelled.

Without signaling and barely reducing his speed, he suddenly turned off the main road onto a dirt one that had a large wooden gate across it.

A heavy chain and a padlock were on the gate along with a sign which read, "Cattle Rustlers Will Be Prosecuted."

Luther got out of the car, leaving the engine running and the musicians finishing the Beethoven piece. He walked to the gate, unlocked the padlock with a key taken from his breast pocket, then moved the heavy gate to the side of the road. After getting back into the car and driving it onto the ranch land, he got out again and reversed the procedure.

As he drove the car along the winding dirt road, Debra felt enveloped by the old oaks on either side. Heavily draped with Spanish moss, they formed a lush canopy over the car.

A golf cart came toward them driven by a very tan, very blond young man wearing only tennis shorts and a baseball cap. He pulled the cart to the side of the road and nodded as they passed.

"One of my boys," Luther stated. "I have about fifteen young folks working on the ranch. I give them little homes to live in, scattered here and there on my land. A few young women, too. Never can figure out who is living with whom. But they're good kids. I have a bunch of those carts to make getting around easier for them."

He turned left and Debra saw a huge rambling ranch house of weathered gray wood next to a small lake. A wide driveway curved past the front entrance to a large three-sided barn. As they drove into the barn structure Debra saw three Jeeps and two vans lined up like horses in stalls. Luther maneuvered the car into an empty stall and gestured to ten golf carts lined up against the side of the barn.

"Gave most of the kids the day off, just like you," he said as he got out of the car. "They like to start partying early on Friday. I just kept a few around to be on patrol."

"Patrol?" Debra questioned. She moved quickly to open the car door before he dashed around to her side.

He was doing just that when he said, "You modern women are too fast for me. Yup, they're on the lookout for rustlers. I had two cattle cut up and carted off just three miles from the ranch house last week. They do it at night, usually . . . the bastards. Please excuse my language."

Luther led the way to the house with Debra walking rapidly to keep pace with his long strides. Her high heels were quickly covered with a film of brown dust.

"Have you ever caught any rustlers in the act?" she asked, as Luther unlocked the double seven-foot wood doors and stepped aside to let her enter first.

"Yup. Strung up four last month," he said with a chuckle as he closed the door behind them.

His joke hardly registered with Debra. She was stunned by the cavernous darkness of his home. She sensed, rather than saw, an extremely large room. Luther walked by her into the dark expanse and she heard his cowboy boots tapping in front of her. She stood quietly, waiting for her eyes to adjust. There was a dim light source in the distance and she saw Luther silhouetted before it. Gradually she could see more: there were dark tall pillars supporting a high beamed ceiling; a very long, narrow dining room table was on her right, and to her left, against the wall, there was an elaborate armoire. She walked closer to it and saw that it contained a six-foot antique mirror surrounded by large wood hooks holding at least ten cowboy hats.

"Well, come on in. Don't be shy," Luther called.

Debra walked toward him past the fat pillars which, she discovered, were made of rough-hewn wood. Several had bales of hay propped against them. She wondered if Luther held barn dances in the huge room.

The light was coming from a fire burning in a large stone fireplace. Luther was poking at it. He indicated with a nod that he wanted her to sit on the couch in front of the fire. She did so, and noticed that the upholstery was torn in several places. Five chairs were also grouped in front of the fire, each with a tree stump next to it to act as a side table.

How very odd this place is, she thought, and how very hot: it was 80 degrees outside and at least 90 degrees by the fire. As if sensing her thoughts, Luther turned from the fireplace and said, "I like it warm in here. These spring days can be tricky: hot all day and then a sudden draft will give you the chills."

Debra had the strap of her open shoulder bag loosely over her arm as she sat on the couch. Suddenly, a sharp yank on the purse made her lean to one side. She gasped and instinctively yanked back. What looked, in the dim light, like a very large cat was rummaging in her purse and making grunting noises. Debra pulled hard on the purse and said "No!" Luther looked up from his fire-tending and, laughing, said, "Stop it, Rumpus!" Then the animal, what she had thought was a cat, pulled its head out of her canvas bag and stared at her. Debra quickly rose from the couch and backed away from the fat creature, leaving her belongings to a mean-looking raccoon.

"Aunt Alice and I have spoiled that critter. But, heck, we found him when he was just a little fellow and now he seems like 'family.' I'll take him into the other room since he's bothering you. I'll get us some iced tea, too." Luther chuckled as he spoke and appeared to be enjoying Debra's discomfort. He picked up the hissing animal and left.

Debra put her makeup and wallet back into the shoulder bag. She found handling her pawed-over and slightly saliva-tainted things distasteful. With a grimace she walked to the heavy curtains near the fireplace and parted them to see the lake. She was surprised to learn that the curtains covered sliding glass doors that led to a screened porch. In the middle of the long porch was a cage at least seven feet high and six feet wide.

Debra was stunned. She suddenly realized how bizarre the whole place was and she longed to be back in her office. She definitely didn't want to know what man-sized beast was also part of Luther's "family."

"How do you like it?"

She hadn't heard Luther's approach and when he spoke next to her, she reacted with a startled cry and spun around toward him. The curtains fell into place again over the glass doors.

"You sure are a jumpy little thing. Here, have this iced tea before we set out."

Debra took the glass from him with a nervous laugh and thanked him. They sat on the torn couch as Luther explained the cage.

"A black bear has been foraging around the ranch. I'm worried that he might go out on the road and be killed. I had my boys build this so we could take him somewhere safer. Now my foreman William tells me we can't go near the old fellow without the state wildlife people involved. Heck."

"Well, I'm relieved to know that the cage won't be used for rustlers," Debra said.

"Darn right. It's too good for them. Bring your glass outside for a minute. I want to introduce you to someone."

Debra followed him across the living room to the front door. She noticed that he picked up a small paper bag from the long table as he walked by it.

Going back out into the sun momentarily blinded Debra and she groped her way down the front steps. Luther led her to the back of the house and then over to the gently sloping bank of the lake.

"Made this lake myself. It was nothing but a tiny little swamp before I brought in the dredging equipment. Of course, I didn't tell the bureaucrats what I did. You need permits to fuss with the aquifer around here. Anyway, I created something pretty and made a nice home for my friend." Luther squatted by the lake and opened the paper bag. He took two marshmallows from it and held them in his outstretched hand.

"What friend?" Debra inquired. Her high heels sank into the mushy ground cover as she walked to where Luther waited.

"You'll see. He'll be here in a second," Luther replied. Then Debra heard a splashing sound from the opposite bank and saw a five-foot alligator gliding toward them. As it approached, Debra began to walk backward. The alligator lifted its head two feet from Luther's outstretched hand and opened its jaws. Luther tossed the two marshmallows into its mouth.

"It could take off your hand!" Debra exclaimed.

"No, he won't. He's known me and my marshmallows since he was a baby. See, he's smiling," Luther said.

"I've been here long enough to know that's the way they always look," Debra countered.

Luther laughed and tossed five more marshmallows to the alligator. Its jaws opened to catch them and snapped shut. Debra didn't find it amusing.

"Sometimes I worry that he might get cavities," Luther said.

They walked back to the car barn after leaving her glass of iced tea by the front door, and Luther helped her into an open Jeep. It was old and made a grinding noise when he put it in gear.

"We're off," he shouted as they lurched forward with a neck-snapping jolt. He left the dirt road just as they passed the ranch house and drove into an open plain of high grass. This ride, Debra soon realized, was nothing like her previous rides with Bobby. Luther obviously relished driving off the road; he grinned as the Jeep bumped over hidden holes and careened through eight-foot-high pampas grass that whipped them as they passed.

The jolting ride was exhilarating to Debra. The area they were in reminded her of locales in African safari films. She had never seen such thick vegetation, much less driven through it. She clutched the side of the Jeep with one hand and braced her body on the seat with the other. Twice, huge herons gave raucous angry cries as they flew up from their disturbed nesting places and flapped their wings over her head.

When the Jeep passed a low swampy area, hundreds of screeching white egrets took flight from thick bushes. Luther pointed out herds of cattle in the distance and showed her flocks of wild turkeys among the trees.

She was hot and worried about her prolonged exposure to the late afternoon sun when suddenly he stopped near a heavily wooded area.

"Let's go into some shade," he suggested. "I'll take you through some of my favorite swamps."

When he turned into the dark jungle the dim light and quiet atmosphere soothed her. They drove slowly through the shallow water around cypress trees with tangled wet roots. She heard soft croaking sounds from hundreds of unseen frogs. Luther seemed to know exactly how deep the swamp water was as he careful steered the Jeep into areas that appeared impassable to Debra.

They came to a marshy lake dotted with wide lily pads. Tall trees loomed on either side and thick vegetation blurred the lake's boundaries. She assumed he would stop and back up, but instead he yelled, "Let's cut across her. This Jeep can handle it!" and he drove into the lake.

The Jeep made small waves on either side as they labored through the water. In the middle of the lake, the engine stopped. The water was above the front of the Jeep and washed over the floorboards. It felt warm and slimy as it lapped at Debra's feet before she drew them up under her on the seat after placing her wet shoes on the seat beside her.

Neither she nor Luther had spoken since entering the lake. She looked at him and saw that his facial wrinkles, which had crinkled in delight during their ride, now drooped into dejected furrows. She realized that he must be feeling embarrassed to have misjudged the water's depth.

"Maybe if we both got out and pushed . . . ?" she asked in an upbeat manner, hoping he'd refuse her offer. She couldn't imagine stepping into heaven-knows-what muck on the bottom.

Luther turned a stricken face to her.

"No, Debra. I won't expose you to water moccasins, alligators, and leeches. I'm real embarrassed and sorry. This was a damned fool thing to do. You just sit right here. I'm going to wade out of this and go for help."

"How far back is the ranch house? How long do you think you'll be gone?" Debra asked.

"Well, let me see. We've been gone about an hour and a half. I'd say we're about five miles from the house. I know the shortcuts, and I'll be back in a jiffy."

"Why don't I go with you? You shouldn't make the walk alone. Maybe, if I'm too heavy to carry, I could swim out." Debra was trying to think clearly. She was torn between her fear of the dark water and its lurking dangers and her fear of being left alone to worry about the old man walking through the difficult terrain without her.

"Little lady, you'd be an easy bundle for a younger man to carry and I sure wish I could do that. As for swimming, there are two reasons I don't want you to: there are indeed disagreeable things in these waters and besides, your clothes are already unsuitable for a jungle trek; it would be worse if you were all wet, too. You just stay right here and keep your legs on the seat. It'll be twilight soon and you'll be a lot safer here, waiting, than walking with me."

Luther slowly eased his lanky body over the Jeep door and into the water. He was at least six feet tall and the muddy water came to his waist. Without saying anything more to Debra he slowly made his way to where they had entered the lake. When he reached the bank he slid several times before finding secure footing. Just before disappearing into the thick tangle of cypress trees he turned and gave Debra a jaunty salute.

She continued to stare at the place where she had last seen him. The sloshing sounds he made as he walked through the swampy area receded. Then there was silence. Her legs, tucked under her, were cramping and she stretched them over the driver's seat. She was grateful she was partially dry and tried not to think of her ruined, wet shoes.

The setting sun highlighted the dense foliage around the lake. It really was quite beautiful, she realized. She had always loved walking through the climate-controlled rain forests in botanical gardens. Even as a child she had been fascinated by lacy ferns and huge banana leaves. She had fantasized about romantic jungle adventures. Well, here she was. Maybe Luther didn't fit her image of a handsome hero, but she was definitely in the middle of a jungle adventure.

Be careful what you wish for, you may get it, she remembered her mother saying.

As twilight arrived the insect sounds and bird calls increased from background noise into a rising crescendo. Debra suddenly realized that her legs and bottom were damp. The Jeep was slowly settling deeper into the murky water.

Debra began to worry in earnest. If Luther became lost, or fell and couldn't walk, who would find him? Or her? Her thoughts were taking a grim turn.

Suddenly there was a loud splashing sound on her right. Of course, she thought, twilight meant feeding time for alligators. She knew that the doors of the sinking Jeep now provided an inadequate barrier between her and whatever swamp creatures decided to slither in. She wondered if loud noises would deter them.

Debra began to sing a half-remembered nursery song. She was halfway through the lullaby when the mosquitoes descended. Suddenly they were in her ears and up her nose. They bit her scalp and dove for her mouth and eyes. They bit her knees, her feet, and her fingers.

Screaming, she yanked off her blouse and batted the mosquito-thick air. It was hopeless.

She put the blouse over her head and face, creating a small, white tent ... a hot, small, white tent inhabited by mosquitoes that bit and bit and bit.

She began to cry, more angry than scared. What the hell was she doing in this ugly, hot place? All her fingers swelled from the concerted attack. She knew that the alligators were really smiling now. They'd wait until the meat was tenderized by the mosquitoes and then cruise over for dinner.

The twilight ended, but not the feeding frenzy. Through the cloth of her blouse, Debra saw a light. Afraid to remove the blouse from her head, fearing what she might see swimming around the Jeep, she slowly lifted some of the material over one eye. Car headlights were approaching. She quickly removed her "tent" and frantically waved it over her head.

"Here I am!" she yelled. No friendly voice answered; there was just the steady engine hum of the vehicle. It stopped on the bank opposite Debra, its headlights hurting her eyes. She heard the car door open and a deep male voice with a heavy Southern accent shouted: "Now don't you worry. I'm going to walk in and get you."

The voice was unfamiliar to Debra. She hastily put on her blouse when she heard the man enter the lake. A large figure blocked out some of the light from the headlights. As the dark shape came nearer, she heard sympathetic murmurings.

"Why, you poor little thing. Poor lost little lady. You're just about eaten alive by skeeters, aren't you?"

Suddenly the stranger loomed next to her. He was very tall with extremely broad shoulders. Very gently she was lifted to a standing position on the Jeep seat with her shoulder bag slung around her neck. The stranger then turned his back.

"Put your arms around my neck and wrap your legs around my middle. I'm going to give you a piggyback ride to my truck."

He smelled of cattle and tobacco. Debra, as she wrapped herself securely against him, realized that his broad back was misshapen. One shoulder was considerably higher than the other.

When they reached the open truck door he positioned himself so that she could slide from his back onto the front seat.

"Now just scoot over to the other side and I'll drive us out of here. I'll worry about that damn fool Jeep tomorrow."

The interior light was on and as she slid over to the passenger side she watched her rescuer get into the truck. He was very tan, near sixty, perhaps, and had long, snow-white hair pulled into a ponytail. When he turned to smile at her she saw beautiful pale blue eyes in a handsome, weather-beaten face.

"My name is William Bearclaw, miss. I'm the foreman on this here ranch and I'm mighty glad I found you. Now just relax and we'll be at the ranch house real soon."

During the drive back through the dark pasture and thick foliage, Debra sat silently. Her body felt as if it were on fire. She tried to concentrate on William's soothing voice as he explained how he found her.

"Mister Luther gave almost everyone the afternoon off, me included. After I drove his Aunt Alice to her sister's home in Tampa, I planned to come back to my place and just take it easy. But then I started thinking about the beehives in the east pasture and I decided to check them. You see, a real smart old black bear discovered our hives about two weeks ago and I put up a fence around them to discourage another raid. Well, shoot, there I was looking at the shambles he had made of my puny effort and who did I see strolling out of the woods but Mister Luther. At first I thought he was Brother Bear, it being twilight and my eyes not so good anymore. But it was Mister Luther. He walked up to me and told me he'd been lost in those woods for a couple of hours. He said he'd left a pretty lady sitting in a swamp somewhere. Well, now, gators and skeeters don't care whether a person's pretty or ugly when they're hungry, so I was real worried. But Mister Luther was plumb worn out and asked me to take him back to the ranch house before I set out for you. When he described that old pond, I had a pretty good idea where you were. Missy, when we get back you'll have some smelly stuff put on those bites and they'll be better by tomorrow. You're going to be jus' fine."

Debra couldn't imagine being "jus' fine." As they neared the ranch house she saw Luther and a tall young woman standing under the porch light. William drove the truck to the front steps and Luther rushed to open her door.

"Debra! What a shame this had to happen! You'll probably hate me and this land now." Luther continued to apologize as he led Debra into the house and then into a large and gloomy kitchen. The woman, dressed in cutoff jeans and a plaid shirt tied at her midriff, walked ahead of them. Luther told Debra to sit at the kitchen table while the woman put a large bowl filled with a pasty substance next to her.

"Sara here is going to put something soothing on those bites and then she'll drive you back to your car. William and I will wait by the fire while she takes care of you." With that, Luther left her in the rough hands of Sara, who stripped off Debra's clothes and slathered her with the ointment.

Neither she nor Debra spoke. As Sara worked on her, Debra heard William and Luther talking quietly outside the kitchen door.

"Mister Luther, that little gal needs to get back in the saddle real soon. She just had a bad experience with this land, and if you want her to work happily on that park land, she'd better have a good experience with it right away."

"Yes, yes, of course. Well, we'll think of something," Luther replied.

"I've been thinking, Mister Luther. I'd like to take her to some of my 'pretty spots' on the park land. Maybe this Sunday after church? I'd be right pleased to help her see the beauty of this land," William said.

Overhearing this offer, Debra's reaction was that the last thing she wanted was another journey through the jungle.

When Luther replied, "Don't you have to fix that fence around the beehives this weekend?" she was relieved.

Then William said, "I can get them fixed up proper tomorrow. I'll be free on Sunday and pleased to help out with this nice lady."

Debra was touched by William's concern and realized that there was a kindly logic to what he said. There had been moments during the afternoon when she had seen the beauty in this tropical wilderness. The swamp, however, had made her feel like a foolish and unwanted intruder.

Their voices faded as they walked to the fireplace. Sara finished smearing on the gooey stuff and helped Debra into an old tan raincoat and a pair of Aunt Alice's slippers. Her damp and soiled office clothes were put in a large garbage bag along with her purse and handed to her. She knew her shoes were history.

Debra was now ready for the long and, if her experience with Sara was any guide, silent drive back to her car.

"My daddy taught me how to lean down from the saddle, pick some wild flowers, and stick them in my hat. Well, since I got this back injury in a rodeo accident, there aren't any more days in the saddle. Here, put these little blue cornflowers in your hat. They match your eyes."

William and Debra were having a beautiful Sunday afternoon. Already he had shown her where a wild mother hog and her babies had made a hog wallow on the park site, and he had lovingly described his favorite flowers by their Indian names. She learned that he was half-Cherokee, half-Irish, and an ex-bronco buster from Texas. After his accident he had wandered down into Florida and hired on as foreman for Luther's uncle. That was twenty-five years ago; when Luther inherited the land, William remained to help him.

That Sunday Debra learned to appreciate the land, and William made sure she was dressed appropriately for it with clothing from the ranch. She wore jeans, old boots of Aunt Alice's, a cotton long-sleeved shirt, a cowboy hat, and a red bandanna around her neck to catch the sweat.

He showed her mystical silent places where very old oak trees created green cathedrals hung with Spanish moss tapestries. They also walked to the place on the park site where he wished his ashes to be scattered: a natural amphitheater with a carpet of flowers encircled by more large oak trees.

Some of the time they rode in one of the ranch's four-wheel-drive vans and sometimes they walked quietly through the lush vegetation. Once, when they walked from a high grass area into a shaded glen, Debra looked into the startled eyes of a large buck with a rack of antlers five feet across. The deer was six feet from her and William. The three of them looked at each other. Then the deer broke his gaze and quickly disappeared into the trees.

"There'll be no hunting on this park. No, sirree, Mister Luther has made sure of that. This park is going to be a place where people can come to learn about the real beauty of Florida. People will hike around nature trails during the day and then gather together in a pretty building set in the trees and listen to pretty music. I'm real excited about the park. Shoot, there ain't nothing for the folks around here to do for fun now. No place to walk and no place for them to meet new friends. Those developments the real estate fellows sell — why, they're real ugly! I could never figure out why they can't build the homes among the trees and palmettos and such. Why do they have to kill all the natural stuff?"

Debra felt a genuine fondness for William and knew that he was "natural stuff" himself. She wondered what would happen to him if Luther ever decided to sell his land to developers.

Debra began to understand the responsibility her job entailed. She was saving three hundred acres of land for the enjoyment and education of the people, and she was excited by the thought. She knew that everything was going to be "jus' fine," as William had said.

Chapter Eight

The early morning light bounced off the canal and onto the white bedroom walls. It made the walls seem to quiver. Lying in bed, Debra had the illusion of floating in warm, clear water. The white ceiling fan made soft swirling sounds. A Gulf breeze was blowing into the canal and it caused the palm fronds near her window to gently clatter.

Debra loved the tropical sounds. At first, shortly after her arrival, she was startled awake every morning at five-thirty by the odd cries, calls, and songs of the birds. Now she could identify and enjoy the early morning conversations of the egrets, herons, willets, and sea gulls.

Swimming slowly to consciousness, she looked around the bedroom, pleased. Her familiar white wicker furniture surrounded her. For years in Los Angeles she had collected and refinished wicker furniture from garage sales and secondhand stores. They had finally found their proper setting.

Debra dressed hurriedly, remembering her busy work schedule. She felt some reluctance in leaving her home; it was the only place in this strange land where she felt really comfortable. Also, she still had boxes to unpack. Her work during the week, such as setting up the Palmetto Park office and fund-raising, usually left her so tired in the evenings that all she could do was to fix a small dinner and go to bed. For two and a half months now, unpacked boxes remained in the garage.

She left the house by the back door that led from the large screened porch (the "Florida Room") with its jungle of potted plants that she had bought, and walked onto the lawn that sloped to her small white dock with its built-in bench on the canal. As she did every morning since discovering them marching across the lawn to the water, she said, "Good morning" to the mother duck and ten ducklings. She also waved to the alligator who floated by the dock waiting for the ducklings' morning swim.

"Hope you don't have any luck today," she called to the alligator. No wonder her elderly neighbors peeked at her from behind their curtains, she thought.

She walked around to the front of the house, pausing to look at the neighbor's bushes laden with azalea flowers. It was into those bushes that the snake had slithered the night of the welcome party. Describing it and the incident at the board meeting the following Monday, she discovered that the snake was poisonous and rare. The directors expressed surprise that it chose her doorstep to make an appearance. Luther said his Aunt Alice, absent from the meeting that day, would call it an "omen," but he hoped Debra wouldn't be so foolish.

She pushed the incident from her mind as she walked quickly to her car parked in the driveway. A film of dew covered it, and she again vowed to clear the garage of boxes so that the car could have a proper stable. The car looked smaller to her this morning, and vulnerable; perhaps, she thought, because the dew dulled its vibrant color. Almost simultaneously two thoughts occurred: the car was closer to the ground and each of the tires was flat. They had been brutally slashed.

———

Two hours later, after being towed to a garage, the car still exhibited its ugly wounds. A mechanic was slowly removing the tires while he waited for his assistant to return with four new ones from a tire store twenty miles away. Debra sat on a rusty metal chair watching the flies (a new generation must have been born during her wait, she mused), sweltering in the May heat, and listening to the steady, slow-paced talk coming from the mechanic.

During the first hour of waiting, after calling her morning appointment to say she would be late, she had talked with him about the Palmetto Park project; now the heat and his slowness lulled her into drowsiness.

"Some folks around here don't put up with these foreign cars. Un-American, they say. Maybe someone seen it sittin' there and got pissed at it."

Debra noted the American flag flying in front of the garage and wondered for the twentieth time how much this was going to cost her. Surely the insurance company would reimburse her, she reasoned.

"Like I said, we don't see many of these around here," he continued. "That's why it don't make no sense for me to stock these kinda tires. Funny how I recognized you right away. I sez to Frank, 'that's the gal from California the papers been talkin' about and she's gonna get us that park', I sez. If you don't mind me saying, your newspaper pictures are right pretty, but they sure don't do you justice."

"Thank you."

"Yup. I tell you this here park you're building is sorely needed. There ain't nothin' to do around here. Yes, sir, we're all lookin' forward to having a place to go to and listen to some music and meet our friends and maybe go on a little walk around some pretty land. It'll sure beat the heck out of hog huntin'." The last slashed tire was finally removed.

"It's nice to hear you talk that way about the park. You know that telethon I told you about? Well, maybe you'll donate a lube job to the first ten people who call in. How about it?" Debra smiled encouragingly at the mechanic as she spoke. Might as well make this morning count for something, she thought.

Before he could answer, the assistant returned in his pickup truck and began unloading the four new tires.

"Hey, Fred! This lady's going to Tampa today and talk Alistair Lake into being on TV. The show's going to be on September first, right here on our cable station. Ain't that something?" The mechanic turned to Debra and asked, "What other sports stars are you going to have?"

He had neatly avoided her question, Debra realized. She was amused by the good will toward the park that people voiced and the avoidance some practiced when it came time to reach into their pockets.

"Our own local Olympian, Johnny Holmes, of course, and probably some golf and tennis pros," Debra answered. She was worried about the telethon, and she wondered why she always created more work for herself. The board of directors would have been satisfied with a typical fund-raiser, perhaps an auction with items donated by local merchants, but she wouldn't have been. "Typical" wasn't a method to use when an organization needed to raise funds quickly. The local cable station had agreed to donate their services; now she needed to convince regional celebrities to appear. If she ever got out of this garage she was going to meet a soccer player and coach who was very popular in the state. Hopefully, he would agree to the plan.

Fifty minutes later, Debra was on Dale Mabry, a heavily congested street in Tampa. She had the directions to Alistair Lake's office taped to her dashboard for easy referral. Her blouse was beginning to stick to her. Although she loved her BMW, its air conditioning unit was built for Bavarian weather, not the tropics, she realized.

With relief she made the turn onto the correct cross street. A half-mile beyond the corner was a practice field. A one-story office building, with the sign "Tampa Bay Smashers," faced the street. Debra drove into a parking lot filled with a large mobile TV van and crewmen. The center of attention was a dazzling specimen of male "beef-cake" dressed in soccer gear. Even from where she had parked Debra was struck by his movie star appearance: his blond hair glowed in the sunlight and his smile was brilliant. She hadn't seen anything like him since Dirk, and that seemed like a very long time ago indeed.

She knew it was the "soccer star," and put on some fresh lipstick before leaving the car. She walked toward him and the crowd of crewmen.

He was talking about an Australian beer in a definite "down under" accent. Abruptly he stopped speaking, looked directly at her, and held up his hand.

"That's it, fellows. My lunch date just arrived."

He walked past the protesting director, who said, "Jeez, man, we've almost got it."

The "star's" answer was firm: "It's past lunch time. Everyone needs a break. I'll be back in an hour and a half."

He didn't take his eyes from Debra as he quickly moved through the cluster of men toward her.

As he approached, every detail of his appearance and every movement of his body pierced her with a sharp, almost painful, awareness. She experienced a strange feeling of inevitability; they were going to be lovers.

"Man! It's hot in here." A fine film of sweat glistened on his naked body as he left the bed to open the shutter. A slight breeze played like gentle fingers over Debra's breasts and down the length of her torso. She smiled to think that even the breeze made love to her when she was with Alistair.

Looking at him silhouetted against the night sky and moon-lit Gulf waters, she caught her breath. He was so beautiful.

They had been meeting two times a week for one month and the fierceness of their lovemaking kept increasing. It was Alistair who suggested the trysting place, a stilt shack on the coastal marshes south of New Harbor. The day after their first meeting, when he agreed to appear in the telethon, he brought her to a cluster of three shacks on a dirt road at the edge of the swampy coast line on the pretext of introducing her to smoked mullet.

An old, weathered man prepared the fish in a large out-door oven which was, along with two picnic tables, his restaurant. After they had eaten, he showed them how he caught the fish. They walked onto a small pier that stretched beyond the swamp into deeper water. There were several stilt houses even farther out into the Gulf waters. The man, proud, he said, to be called a "Cracker," flung a heavy, round net with small metal weights around its circumference into the water. It landed in a perfect circle, and when he pulled it out of the water it was filled with flipping silver fish.

It was the old man who told them that one of the stilt houses could be rented by fishermen eager to live over the Gulf water and cast their lines from its porch. A small boat was available to row from the rickety pier to the house. The place was perfect for them. Debra wanted this gorgeous, sensual man, but she didn't want anyone in Palmetto County to know how she felt. Her position was too vulnerable to be tainted by the aura of lust that surrounded her and Alistair. Perhaps, she thought, her reluctance to acknowledge their relationship was because she knew that they would probably never move beyond lust to deeper feelings.

Alistair turned from the window and, getting back in bed, pulled Debra toward him. While his expert fingers intimately explored her, he spoke softly in her ear. She found it very difficult to concentrate on what he was saying.

"Still afraid to tell people we're 'dating,' Debra? Do you think those good ol' boys would be shocked? Sweet thing, those fellows on your board are probably up to their eyeballs in hanky-panky. I doubt that anything could shock them."

He moved his mouth to her breast. Debra's breathing quickened, and she answered in short, breathy phrases.

"They're men . . . they've been here a long time ... I'm a woman . . . and an outsider. And I'd lose my credibility . . . if they started imagining . . . me in bed with you."

He lifted his head and gazed at her innocently with his twinkling blue eyes.

"Maybe your 'credibility' for some things, luv, but not for others."

His mouth moved lower on her body and he began to further arouse her. Just as she was about to explode, he left her trembling on the bed.

"Don't worry. I'll take care of you, and me, soon. A little sexual tension is good. Want a drink?"

"A 'little' tension? And, no, thank you," she gasped. She watched him hungrily as he walked to the trapdoor on the floor of the shack. He crouched over it, opened it, and pulled up a long rope. A six-pack of beer was tied to it. Salt water dripped off the cans and splashed down into the water seven feet below. He twisted off a can and lowered the rest back into the cool water. Instead of returning to Debra, he took the beer outside to the narrow porch which encircled the small hut. She watched his fluid movements as he took a deep swallow and leaned on the porch railing.

"Come back to bed, Alistair," she said, hoping that her voice didn't betray her need.

He ignored her request. "When are you going to Tallahassee, Debra?"

"Next week. The grant request is complete and Bobby's father has lined up two introductions for me. Bobby's going, too. I have to try it, Alistair. Donations are coming in for the roads, but no one, so far, has contributed the five hundred thousand dollars we need for the Nature Center."

"So Bobby's going up there, too, is he?" Alistair walked across the room to the bed and looked down at her while slowly rolling the cold beer can across his tanned chest.

"Debra, I've been thinking about Bobby and the other developers around here. Seems to me they might need someplace to put their money. The 'Smashers' need money. Game attendance has fallen. You know, they have me not only playing and coaching; they have me promoting the team, too. Why don't you put in a good word with Bobby? Hell, I don't know if he'd make any money from his investment, but it might give him a tax write-off. If I got a few of those high rollers involved, I wouldn't have to worry about scaling down my lifestyle."

"You mean we could keep this 'palace?'" she laughed. Then she added, "It would be better if you hustled them yourself, you conniving Aussie. Talk to them during the planning meetings for the telethon."

"Maybe I will . . . since you won't. I'm starving. Guess I'll dress and get us some food. Just lie there on the bed, luv, and think about what I'm going to do when I get back."

"I think I've had my fill of smoked mullet, though," she said.

"Old Herb was cooking some sea chowder when we arrived. How's that sound?" he asked as he reached under the bed, found his tennis shorts, and quickly put them on.

When she answered, "Fine," he kissed her and descended the ladder down to the rowboat they kept tied to one of the stilts. She heard the oars being put into the water and then his voice was floating over the water as he rowed away.

"Now don't go shimmying down that trapdoor rope while I'm gone. I've got plans for you. Besides, a shark might find out just how good you taste."

Smiling, Debra thought, *Don't worry, I'm staying right here ... at least for another hour or so*. She always dreaded the late night drive, alone, back to her home. Invariably, as the time to leave their bed approached, she began to think about work. The transition between her work life and her love life wasn't easy. Her mind started racing, filled with the thoughts of what she had to do at the office before leaving for Tallahassee. She was grateful for Betty Lou; her cheerful assistant never complained about the mounds of paperwork.

Debra was aware that a successful fund-raising trip to Tallahassee was a long shot. Except for occasional Department of Education grants given to the college, Palmetto County never received state money. They had never tried to approach their legislators. Everyone on the board had been disbelieving when she told them about the proposal and asked them to approve the endeavor. They voted to let her proceed, but the general attitude was one of condescension. She couldn't understand why, except for Johnny, Joe and Martha (and Alice when she "tuned in"), most of the men weren't concerned about the October fifteenth deed restriction. Stanley kept saying not to worry; he'd get the deadline on construction extended. But what if he didn't? Debra asked herself. She had to try for state money to begin the Nature Center. Once it was part of Phase One, and people were using the park, she and the board could begin a fund-raising campaign for the Cultural Center. Private, local support for the park would be easier once state money was involved; people would believe in the park. Debra looked around the fishing shack and laughed aloud. Who would have believed that, in the space of four months, she'd be stranded in a swamp and involved with an Australian in a stilt house over the Gulf?

"It's a far, far better thing I do, than I have ever done before." She laughed when she said the quote aloud, not remembering if it was exact or not, but realized that it reflected how she felt. She liked this strange life working for the "good of the people." As long as she had moments, such as now, when she could imagine herself as a tropical character in a Somerset Maugham novel, she'd be all right.

The Gulf was very quiet. Occasionally she heard soft splashing sounds caused by the gentle tide lapping against the stilts. Or maybe they were the sounds of small fish jumping away from a shark hunting for his dinner, she thought. The image of a cruising shark destroyed her tranquil mood. Sensing a menace in the calm, tropical night, she wanted Alistair next to her. Then she heard the rhythmic sound of the oars and relaxed again.

We have at least two more hours, she thought.

Chapter Nine

T he fog lay in thick, random patches. Sometimes the speeding car would find itself in a gray-white world without other objects, and then it would emerge into a country scene lit by the rising sun before plunging back into the void.

He was driving too fast. She had experienced his recklessness before, of course, and probably should have found an excuse to refuse his offer this morning, but it had seemed reasonable and convenient to have him take her to the small county airport. Thankfully, he had put the convertible's top up.

"There's so much moisture in these swamps and low pasture lands that this early morning fog happens all the time . . . just about at sunrise, like now. Don't you worry, either; I'm used to this road and I've driven it in worse fog than this." Luther took the curves without hesitation while holding a mug of coffee in one large hand.

Debra held her half-full Styrofoam cup with both hands and sat stiffly upright, afraid that the next curve or bump would cause the coffee to splash onto her pale gray linen suit.

"We have ground fog like this in California, too, in the valleys, mostly. It's called 'tule fog' after the grasses in the Central

Valley region. Sometimes thirty or more cars would pile on top of each other on the freeways because of it," she said. Now maybe the old guy would slow down, she thought.

"Thirty cars or more, you say. No danger of that here. In the early morning the only thing on the road besides a few ranchers like me might be a stray cow. How's the coffee?"

"Fine," she replied, "thank you for bringing it . . . and thank you for driving me to the airport. I have no idea where it is and this fog wouldn't have helped me find it." As she spoke she noticed that they were in a particularly dense patch and that Luther hadn't reduced his speed.

"Well, you're very welcome for both. I like to think of myself as an old Southern gentleman and my self-image got a wee bit tarnished when I stranded you in that swamp. I'm still trying to make up for that." His smile rearranged many of the wrinkles on his profile when he heard Debra murmur her protest that it really had been forgotten.

"Anyway," he continued, "I'm used to getting up at five a.m. Now tell me, how did you talk Frank into letting you and Bobby take his plane to Tallahassee?" With his question he turned to look at Debra, but she was staring ahead with a startled look on her face. Yellow lights had suddenly appeared directly in front of their car.

"Ahead!" Debra cried. Luther swung the car into the left lane to avoid hitting what appeared to be a stationary, squat tower with lights. Driving by it, Luther honked the horn and muttered, "That's the damnedest fool thing . . . moving farm equipment out into the road in this fog."

Debra took a deep breath before answering his question about the plane. "Bobby said to call Frank," she replied. "He's a friend of his, and Bobby knew he'd understand the importance of this fund-raising trip to Tallahassee. Apparently, he and Bobby and Frank's pilot take hunting trips in the plane.

Frank knows the park organization doesn't have enough money to take commercial flights out of Tampa, so he donated the use of his company plane and pilot and said we could use both in the future, too. We had a very nice phone conversation. I told him to submit the cost of everything and I'd send him an in-kind contribution receipt."

"There are plenty of those little private planes and small airstrips around here. Real estate developers find that it's an easy way to learn the land." Luther took a sip from his coffee mug but kept his eyes on the road as he continued talking. "Some folks say those little planes are used for more than real estate wheeling and dealing, too."

"You mean all those media stories about Florida's drug trafficking?" Debra asked.

Luther nodded and gave a short laugh. "The real world isn't on film and those news guys exaggerate everything," he paused and then continued: "I'll tell you what is real, though: our five o'clock thunderstorms during the summer. You just make sure you take off from Tallahassee before they hit. Every year we have inexperienced Northerners who fly their private planes down here and try to outrun those big thunderheads that pile up in the east between four and five in the afternoon. Frank's pilot is a local boy, so you just listen to him and leave when he tells you to, okay?"

Debra nodded when he glanced at her, wishing that the fog would lift and this interminable ride end. Luther was certainly being unusually talkative, she thought.

As if reading her thoughts, Luther said, "For a quiet old fellow, I'm sure talking up a storm today. Guess I'm pleased that things are starting to move in this county. Having you here to promote the park project is going to draw attention to our needs in this area. Now I don't want you to be disappointed if those fellows up there in the capital don't just hand over the state funds to help the park. These things take time, you know. But while you're there you can apply that enthusiasm to something else that will help the park."

"What's that, Luther?" Debra replied quickly, afraid that he would look at her for her response and take his eyes from the road again.

"We have about five more minutes until we get to the airport, so listen carefully," he said, and then paused while he sipped his coffee again. Debra also sipped her lukewarm coffee and looked out the side window. She saw a very fat, very dead armadillo by the side of the road, with a turkey vulture trying to pick at it through its armor. For once she was glad Luther was driving fast. Seeing the roadside drama made her realize that the fog was slowly lifting. Debra shifted her attention back to Luther and his rambling conversation.

"... and now old Stephenson has agreed to give his ranch land that fronts the proposed bypass, too. So with my right-of-way guaranteed, and his, the state can't ignore the logic of a bypass state road running parallel to Highway 19 from the counties south of our county straight through to the north. Do you realize what wonderful access the park will have? The bypass will have an exit less than half a mile from its entrance. What I'm saying is this: I have a friend in the State Department of Transportation. I called him yesterday and told him we had Stephenson's agreement, and that you were going to be up there pitching the park project. What this friend and I want you to do is explain the park project to a few other fellows in D.O.T. Convince them that without the bypass we'd have traffic problems when the park opens. Tell them that the park is a sure thing, of course. Here's his name." Luther put his coffee mug on the dashboard and handed Debra a slip of paper from his breast pocket. "Call him when you're through with the legislators and set up some time for a quick presentation. Got it?"

"Sure. It'll be a tight schedule, but I'll be glad to talk with them. I heard Harvey Brown talking about the proposed bypass after the last board meeting. He said it would make the land more valuable." Debra realized that she was bored with the talk of roads and land deals and chided herself for her lack of enthusiasm. It was all part of being a member of this community. Anything that was related to "her" park project should be important, she thought. However, she longed for conversations about films and music and dance and . . . her thoughts began to drift until Luther spoke.

"Here we are. Looks like Bobby's already here." He swung the car into a small parking lot next to a Quonset hut. The entrance sign read: "Palmetto County Airport." Bobby's silver Jaguar blended eerily with the drifting remnants of fog.

Luther parked his car next to the Jaguar and took Debra's briefcase from the back seat as she got out of the car. The air was heavy with warm moisture and smelled of clean wet grass. It was very quiet. A light blinked from a high tower next to the Quonset hut as they walked to the entrance.

Luther, as usual, made a flourish of opening the door for her. As they entered they were assaulted by laughter and cigarette smoke. Five men were standing in the neon-lit room drinking coffee from Styrofoam cups. It was obvious that they were reacting to a punch line. Bobby was the only one dressed in a suit. Two of the men wore jeans and short-sleeved shirts, while the other two wore old Army fatigues. All the men were in their early thirties, and the way they were standing indicated that Bobby was the center of attention.

Turning toward Debra and Luther, Bobby said, "Good mornin', Debra! Ready to blow this Popsicle stand and get some money? How're you doing, Luther?"

Luther shook everyone's hand and introduced Debra to the group. Then, saying he had to get back to the ranch, he handed Debra's briefcase to her, tipped his Stetson and left the building.

The other men also left, saying, "See you later, Bobby," and "Nice to meet you, Debra," and "Good luck in Tallahassee." Debra watched through the open door as three of the men went into a large hangar. The fourth went into a small office at one end of the Quonset hut. Standing next to Bobby, Debra noticed that he showed no signs of that not-quite-awake look most people, she included, evidenced at six a.m. He was perfectly groomed and his curly blond hair fell over his forehead in studied casualness. Bobby lit one cigarette after another as they waited for the pilot. His eyes moved restlessly around the small terminal.

"Are you nervous about flying, Bobby?" Debra inquired.

"Me? No, I just want to get going. Tallahassee is a wild place with lots of action. I'm primed for it. You know, once we get up there and start running from office to office, we're going to need lots of caffeine to keep us going ... or something else."

"No more coffee for me. I'm tense enough right now worrying about what I'm going to say to those fellows. Thanks, Bobby, for having your dad arrange the meeting with the Senate Appropriations Committee chairman," Debra said.

Bobby didn't acknowledge her thanks. He moved closer to her and put his hand on her shoulder.

"It's not good to be tense, Debra. Those fellows up there can sense desperation a mile away . . . and when they do it gives them the upper hand. How about something that will make you feel on top of everything? Loose and easy. Come on, it'll be a boring flight without some help."

His smile was bright and his physical energy intense. Debra felt attracted to him. But he was a member of the board of directors — her employer, really. Last week she had told Alistair that she had to be very careful around these men and she knew she was right. Now, under these harsh lights, Bobby was making the first overt move. Although his face, energy, and body language said "sex," his words said "drugs."

Debra's stomach knotted as she wondered how to handle the situation gracefully. Bobby was still looking at her intently and smiling.

"No, thanks, Bobby. Let's celebrate with some champagne later if things go well in Tallahassee, okay?" Debra replied. She put her hand on his arm lightly and continued, "Now tell me about our pilot. Tell me that he's the best you've ever flown with."

———— ◆ ————

Tommy Thompson had flown in Vietnam. He was a burned-out veteran of twenty-two when he returned to Palmetto County, and all he had wanted to do for several years afterwards was to take care of the family farm and to mend his mind along with the fences. After a few years he felt better and accepted Frank Marillo's job offer. Frank needed a company pilot to take prospective buyers on aerial tours of his developments throughout Florida. Tommy needed to fly again. He was a good pilot and a simple, rather homely, young man. On this particular June day he was happy. The young woman sitting next to him in the copilot's seat was pretty and cheerful. Her obvious pleasure in seeing Florida from the air made him feel generous — he was giving her the gift of the scenery. Tommy glanced at her and knew that the talk about her was right: she wasn't at all "stuck-up"—she was nice.

"How green it is!" exclaimed Debra, "and I never knew there were so many lakes and rivers. They look like silver plates and ribbons from up here!"

To Debra the land below appeared uninhabited, but she knew that her impression was based on a comparison to Southern California.

Bobby was quiet in the back seat during the two-hour flight. Just before landing in Tallahassee, Debra looked back and saw that he was asleep. He looked like an innocent little boy.

The small airport was packed with people. Most of them were anxious-looking middle-aged men wearing dark polyester suits and carrying briefcases. Bobby, still a little groggy from sleep, dismissed them all as "a bunch of hyperthyroid lobbyists." Debra knew that during the few months of the legislative session decisions involving millions of dollars would be made. Walking through the crowd to get a cab, she realized that the excitement she felt from the surrounding people was because they were players in a high-stakes game.

The ride into the capital took them down tree-lined boulevards and past old Southern homes with pillars and verandas. New office buildings had been built to look like Southern mansions. *Robert E. Lee could have lived happily in the Barnett Bank*, Debra thought.

The cab driver told them that most of the year the place slumbered and its small population went about its business. Then, for a few months in the spring, the pace was hectic with the influx of political people: the traffic was chaotic, and the bars, the restaurants, and the taxi cab business flourished.

They took Tommy to a Cajun restaurant run by an exairman buddy of the pilot's. He would spend the day there until they all met at the airport at three o'clock. Bobby and Debra got out of the cab at the steps of the Senate Office Building. It was now nine a.m., and the Georgian buildings that formed the governmental complex were already open for business. Secretaries rushed by with flat cartons filled with covered Styrofoam coffee cups. Security guards stood by the large entrances to each building. The people hurrying from one building to the next avoided the shortest route across the brick courtyard. It was already shimmering with heat. Bobby and Debra, along with everyone else, walked next to the buildings in the shade of the overhanging porticos.

Debra knew that linen was supposed to be smart apparel in the tropics, but she was beginning to believe it was a myth. Her gray suit was already wrinkled before the first meeting of the day. It occurred to her that since coming to Florida she had spent an inordinate amount of time worrying about wrinkled clothes, limp hair, and perspiration. It was impossible to look crisp and efficient in this heat and humidity.

Their first meeting was with the chairman of the Senate Appropriations Committee. Senator Grizzard had represented a cluster of counties along the west coast of Florida for twenty-five years. As Debra walked with Bobby along the narrow interior corridors of the Senate Office Building she silently rehearsed what she would say to this good ol' boy of legendary proportions. It was because of his friendship with Bobby's father that he had granted them a fifteen-minute interview, and she had to make those minutes count.

The office they entered was filled with male lobbyists. Bobby stayed by the door as Debra approached the receptionist's desk. The woman had teased red hair and wore violently green eye shadow. Her hard appearance clashed with the frilly flowered summer dress she wore. She and Debra were the only women in the crowded office. Debra identified herself and Bobby and told the woman that they had a nine- fifteen appointment with the senator. The woman glanced up briefly from her work and then, looking at the papers again, told Debra, "Have a seat and wait, please."

There were no seats. Whatever seats had once been available were taken by men busily shuffling papers. They were reading proposals that seemed twice the size of the one she carried. Other men were leaning against the walls and some had propped themselves up against a large bookcase. Most of the men were quiet. Debra noticed that they looked at a secretary as she came through the waiting area on her way to the hall. The men smiled at the secretary and some called a greeting. A narrow corridor led from the left of the receptionist's desk and ended in a room filled with more desks and secretaries. Glancing down the corridor, Debra could see that each desk had a floral arrangement on it. An intense young man in an ill-fitting light blue suit got up from his chair, left his briefcase on it, and walked over to the receptionist. He smiled ingratiatingly at the top of her head as she continued to sort through papers.

"Sherry, I've been here since the doors opened. Last night at Bennigan's you said that the senator would have some time for me this morning," he pleaded.

Without looking up at him, Sherry replied, "Sorry. He's been tied up in conference since seven-thirty."

As the man walked back to his chair Debra noticed that Bobby was no longer lingering by the office door. She walked through the growing crowd of lobbyists into the outside hall to find him. She realized that part of the game plan of Tallahassee was to make friends with the secretaries that worked for the legislators. She surmised that the floral arrangements were probably from the lobbyists. The young women must have a pretty full social life during the session, Debra thought. She also realized that her gender prevented her from playing that particular game.

Bobby was not in the hall. One of the unmarked doors in the hallway, on the same side as the senator's office, was slightly ajar. She heard laughter coming from behind it and then Bobby's drawling voice saying something about daisies.

Debra opened the door wider and saw Bobby and two young women laughing. As she walked into the room she heard Bobby say, "Yes, ma'am, I've always wanted to bury my face in a field of daisies." The woman he was looking at was young, blond, pink-faced, forty pounds overweight, and wore a daisy print blouse stretched across her ample bosom.

Sensing someone standing in the doorway, Bobby turned to Debra and said, "Hi, there. Debra, I'd like you to meet Susie and Pauline. The senator will see us in a minute and this is a much nicer place to wait."

The two women were still glowing from Bobby's attention and smiled at Debra as she entered. A door opened behind the daisy-bloused secretary and a massive figure filled the door frame.

"Well, Bobby, I see you've found the way I sneak in and out." His voice rolled over them. Debra smiled at the vision of this man trying to sneak anywhere.

"Have you corrupted my girls yet?" he continued. "I hope so. I've been trying to think of a way to warm them up. Maybe the scent of you will get their juices flowing."

The senator, and surely this was he, Debra thought, wore a wrinkled dark blue suit, a white shirt, and a stained tie. He had white shaggy hair and an equally shaggy mustache which contained evidence of pastry. As he spoke his many chins wobbled. Debra realized that, as she was forming a first impression, he was also scrutinizing her. It was not a comfortable feeling to be the target of his shrewd look.

"Come on over here, lady. I know you're Debra Price, and I want to shake your hand and feel some California flesh."

Debra walked over to the senator and firmly shook his large hand.

"It's a pleasure to meet you, Senator. I want to feel you, also . . . your legislative strength is legendary," Debra replied.

Looking at Bobby, the senator chuckled, "Guess you're not a wimp anymore, boy, if you're working with the likes of this one. Both of you — come on in."

The senator walked ahead of them to his massive wood desk and sat in one of the largest upholstered chairs Debra had ever seen. On either side of the desk, standing on the floor, were two flags — one Confederate, one American. One wall was all glass, providing an overview of the governmental complex. There was a telescope mounted on the floor next to the window.

Seeing Debra glance at it, the senator said, "People wonder how I stay on top of things, how I know what's happening around here. Well, by God, I just stay right here in my office, look through that thing, and read lips. Hell, I collect good blackmail material, let me tell you, by peeking into some of those offices."

Debra knew he was joking, but his comments gave credence to the talk that this powerful man seemed to mysteriously know everything before it was general knowledge.

Bobby and Debra sat in leather chairs facing the senator and she leaned forward to place the Nature Center proposal on his desk.

Without looking at the proposal, the senator said to Debra, "I got my hands on your proposal last week, so let's not waste time going over its budget and all the research you compiled. You just tell me why the hell, in a legislative session where money is so damned tight and everyone else is hounding me to support their projects, I should try to help your group."

"Because during the last election, when you retained your seat, it was Palmetto County — not the metropolitan counties south of us — that gave you the winning edge, and because

Palmetto County has never asked for anything in return — not until now," Debra replied. She saw both men's faces go suddenly still. After a slight pause, she continued, "and because it's some of the prettiest Florida land anywhere in your district and we're trying to keep it that way. There are bored and lonely retirees in our county. They're disillusioned with their dreams of a tropical retirement. All they see around them are poorly built housing developments. The people of Palmetto should have a place where they can see the natural beauty of rural Florida. They need to meet new friends in an environment other than a shopping mall." Debra paused, then took a deep breath, and continued, "This Nature Center, Senator, is only the start. I was brought here to use my arts education training to plan and promote an educational and cultural center for the people, and I believe, along with a lot of other people down there, that it's going to exist. There's going to be an amphitheater for outdoor concerts and a building for indoor entertainment and conventions. It's about time someone besides real estate developers started enjoying Palmetto County. I think you should seriously consider being the legislator who goes on record as making it all happen."

Debra stopped speaking and realized that she could have easily blown the funding request by her frankness.

"Well, now. Well, well. Aren't you something." The senator spoke slowly as he clipped off the tip of a cigar. "Well, well. Bobby, you still here? And if you are, are you wishing you were somewhere else? Speak, boy."

Bobby appeared perfectly at ease. His legs were crossed and his hands were folded on his knee.

"The only thing I have to say, Senator, is that I don't think Dad would like the reference to 'poorly built housing developments.' Other than that . . . well, she said what a lot of the folks feel," Bobby answered.

"You feel that way about it, Bobby? You and the boys, you all behind this park idea? You fellows down there sometimes play by your own rules. You have your own way of doing things. Are you going to support this thing with more than just nodding your pretty head, Bobby boy?"

"Why sure, Senator. Hell, it might be good for business," Bobby replied with a laugh.

"Well, I'll tell you what, you two: I think I can put in a measly five hundred thousand dollars somewhere in the Senate's appropriations budget. I can't speak for the House side, obviously. I have another little worry: I'm sure as hell not going to go out on some limb just to have this project die on the vine because the boys down there in Palmetto County lose interest in it. This little lady says she speaks for the people and I believe her. I also believe that there's no stopping her. So, I'll see what I can do."

The senator leaned over the desk toward Debra and said, "But there's a bottom line to this deal, my pretty friend. I expect something in return. I expect you to have dinner with me next time I'm in your area, and I'll expect you to be mighty grateful for my help."

Debra knew he wasn't serious about the payback. She also knew he had just committed himself to help the project get the funding. She got up from her chair and leaned across his desk to shake his hand.

"Thank you, Senator. I'm aware that I'll owe you one and so will the people of Palmetto County," she said.

Bobby stood, too, and shook the senator's hand to thank him.

"Who's next on your schedule?" the senator asked Debra.

"We're going to Representative Goodell's office and try to see him before noon. His secretary told Bobby's father that he had some time," she replied.

"She was wrong. The House is in session this morning, and since he's their chairman of Appropriations, I imagine he's right in the thick of it. Tell you what I'll do. I'll write a note to him that you can have a page deliver. That'll bring him off the floor and into your arms." Senator Grizzard was writing something on a pad of paper.

"I can do that? Have him called out?" Debra asked.

"You can't. He could care less about you, frankly. Or your project. The note's from me, saying that I want to talk to him about funding the project and that I want him to meet you. He'll leave the floor. Believe me, when he sees you, he won't be too disappointed I'm not there." The senator laughed and gave Debra the note.

"What are you going to be doing, Bobby? This lady can handle Goodell by herself," the senator said.

"Oh. Well . . . maybe I'll drop by Ed Haze's office and say 'hello,'" Bobby replied.

"Good idea, boy. You find out for me how the hell he's managed to be Commissioner of Agriculture for thirty-five years. I might need a few tips on how to extend my time. Ed plays it pretty cozy with some of your ranchers down there, I hear. Maybe they bankroll him more than we know, right, Bobby?" the senator asked.

"I wouldn't know about that, sir. I just know that Ed has been a family friend for over twenty years. He's never missed one of our annual barbecues. He and Luther and Dad are going fishing next month. He's 'family,' Senator."

"Is he giving you any tips on how to harvest your marijuana fields, boy?" The senator laughed, but he looked intently at Bobby.

"Hell, yes, Senator. Just last month he sent down two agriculture experts from the University to give me advice," Bobby joked.

"Good. I like to see 'family' helping each other. Now you two run along. I've said I'd help out and I will. You probably know that funding requests have to get through both the House and the Senate, with final approval resting with the Governor. Give me a call next week, Debra, and I may be able to give you some idea of the lay of the land." The senator shook their hands again before Bobby and Debra left.

In the narrow corridor outside the office, Debra gave Bobby a quick hug and exclaimed, "I think we did it! Maybe, just maybe, we can celebrate! If he has half the influence people say he has, we can count the money!"

Bobby stood impassively and let Debra hug him. Then he said, "He's right, Debra, you're 'something else.' No one else could have done what you did. Sure as hell, this is going to surprise a few people. With him wound around your little finger, how can you lose?"

"Bobby! It's not because of me; it's because of the timely aspect of the project. It's perfect for him to get behind it. He needs to do something for Palmetto County, and this park project is worthwhile." Debra was surprised that Bobby wasn't excited. She wondered if the senator's attitude toward him had upset Bobby. She also wondered who had put the proposal into the senator's hand before her arrival. Probably Joe had arranged it through the "contacts" he always mentioned, she mused. She said a silent, *Thank you, Joe.*

"Sure. Okay. You go over to the House side with that note and I'll go see Ed and maybe have a few drinks with him. Meet me at The Saloon on Main Street at two. We'll get a cab back to the airport. See you later, kid." Bobby turned and walked away.

Debra was disappointed by his attitude but decided not to let it bother her. It had happened before. Business triumphs had been construed, in some men's minds, as her sexual triumphs. She had to be content with the personal knowledge that it was a job well done. The right preparations, the reasonable budget, the concisely written presentation . . . those aspects made the project solid.

Debra took the Senate elevators to the ground floor and asked a security guard for directions to the House. Once there, she found the small office where the pages gathered to pick up messages. She gave the senator's note to one of the young male pages and watched as he hurried away with it. Her heart was beating quickly and her palms felt moist as she stood near the wide oak-paneled double doors that led onto the floor of the House. She had seen newspaper photographs of Representative Goodell and knew to expect a tall, thin man with a gray crew cut and military posture. The doors opened and a squat man hurried out. He bumped into Debra without an apology and disappeared down an adjacent corridor. She recognized him as the representative who had been implicated in a land scandal near Miami. The newspapers stated that he was linked to the East Coast Mafia, she remembered.

The doors opened again and Representative Goodell stepped out and quickly scanned the area. He immediately looked irritated. Debra walked over to him, thinking that he was very different from Senator Grizzard. He was cold, with no pretense of back-slapping familiarity.

"Hello, Representative Goodell. I'm Debra Price. Senator Grizzard wanted me to talk with you as soon as possible," she said, and extended her hand.

"Where's the senator?" he asked, without acknowledging her greeting or her extended hand. Not waiting for her reply, he continued, "I see. This is just like him. All right, I have exactly four minutes. Tell me why I should be interested in what you have to say. Debra? Right?"

"Yes. I'm Debra and I'm handing you a grant request for five hundred thousand dollars for a Nature Center for Palmetto

County. We need a park and this is the first step in developing the donated park land. We need something nice for our county for a change. Please read the proposal, sir, and support it. Palmetto County has never had a relatively large appropriations item in the state budget, just occasional small grants for our community college. The people of Palmetto figure it's about time we asked for more. Senator Grizzard apparently thinks so, too. As Chairman of House Appropriations you could help us. Please." Debra knew her four minutes were almost over and stopped speaking.

"You're new up here, aren't you? Hasn't anyone told you that you have to go through the proper channels? First you submit your proposal to the Department of Education or, maybe in this case, the Department of Parks and Recreation. Then they submit it with their recommendations to the House and Senate for consideration," he said.

"Sir, I've been told that, but I was also told that another approach could be used and that was to go directly to the decision-makers such as yourself and Senator Grizzard. Yes, I'm new at this, but I believe in this project. We're in a hurry down there in Palmetto County, sir," Debra replied.

"You're taking a big chance, miss. You're taking another gamble right now by counting on my good humor. I know Grizzard set you up for this, but nevertheless, you're taking a chance." Representative Goodell took the proposal from her hand and continued speaking, "I'll have my staff go over this and someone may get back to you. Now excuse me." He started to walk back to the double doors and then turned to speak to Debra again: "Either you or this proposal or both must be very good if Grizzard means what he says in this note."

"Please read the proposal. It's good, and the time is right for it," Debra answered.

"We'll see." Representative Goodell turned quickly and went into the chamber.

Debra took a deep breath and thought, again, how different the two chairmen were. Although Goodell appeared formidable, she knew that Grizzard held the power.

Her conversations with the two men had tired her. She wanted to go somewhere quiet and think about what had happened that morning. Instead, she walked over to a bank of telephones to call Luther's friend at the Department of Transportation. She had promised Luther that she would promote the bypass and its tie-in with the park project, and she wanted to get it over with.

Fortunately, Joe Slaughter, Luther's friend, was in his office and said he'd assemble a few other men at D.O.T. for a quick presentation.

Debra walked the three blocks to the Department of Transportation building and felt the heat drain her remaining energy. The nondescript-looking men waiting for her in the meeting room were polite. All of them wore short-sleeved white shirts with pens in their breast pockets. Debra summoned enthusiasm for the park project by emphasizing Senator Grizzard's verbal support. She knew that if she presented the park as a "sure bet," the chances of the Department allocating money for the bypass were greater. After her fifteen-minute presentation she knew she had them believing in the park, as well as considering the access problems they might face if the bypass was not in place by the park's completion date.

———◆———

The heat hit her again when she left the Department building. Its increased intensity was overwhelming. It seemed to pound on her head, wanting her to sink into the cement sidewalk.

It was one o'clock and few people were moving anywhere. Everyone had found an air-conditioned place to eat lunch, drink, and lobby for their projects. Debra didn't know where to go, but she knew she had to find a destination soon or she would simply stop and let the heat have its way with her.

She passed under tall oak trees with still leaves and dripping Spanish moss and walked by old homes with empty porches. The town was a curious mix of old residential areas and government buildings, but Debra's interest was subdued by the 100-degree, humid heat.

Several side streets veered from the main complex of government buildings. Debra chose one at random, hoping that some enterprising person had placed a restaurant on it.

They had. The sign read, "The Old Eatery." She entered the small restaurant and felt a wave of air-conditioned coolness wash over her. The overhead fans mixed cigarette smoke with snatches of conversation and dispersed both throughout the crowded room. A raucous voice immediately greeted Debra's entrance.

"Debra! Over here!"

Martha Weil was the last member of one of the numerous German families that had settled in Palmetto County many generations ago. Debra's first encounter with her had been at the welcome party Bobby had arranged when Debra had first arrived. Debra's initial impression of Martha had not been flattering, nor had subsequent ones. She appeared drunk most of the time, except for the weekly eight a.m. meetings of the Palmetto Park board of directors. At the meetings she was usually quiet.

As Debra approached Martha's table in response to her greeting, she saw that Martha was alone; her round face was flushed, and she looked older than her forty-five years. However, if Martha was distressed in any way there was no indication of it when she smiled at Debra.

"How did it go? I've been wondering how you and Bobby did with your meetings. What's the response to the request?" Martha didn't pause during her questions while she cleared the chair next to hers of papers, a large straw hat, and a briefcase.

Debra sat down and sighed. Martha, misinterpreting, looked at Debra sympathetically and continued talking.

"Well, really, you have to admit that it was a real long shot, honey. Why would the fellows in this town care about Palmetto County? I supported the idea of you coming up here because maybe next year, or the year after that, you can try again. Personally, I think we have to be masochists to deal with these bastards. Why did I agree to represent the Board of Realtors up here? Dumb."

Debra looked at Martha's pretty, wide face and saw her honest concern for the first time.

"Martha! I think maybe we did get the funding! Senator Grizzard supports it and you know what that means!" Debra grinned and put her hand on Martha's arm. Martha looked suddenly disoriented. Debra gave two quick pats to her arm and continued, "It's true. Bobby couldn't believe it either. The senator liked the idea. He said he'd do what he could. The wheels are turning, and we could have an answer in a week or so."

"You're not kidding me, are you, child?" Martha looked closely at Debra and then yelled, "Hurrah! Where's that cute little son-of-a-bitch, Bobby? We should all celebrate."

"I'm meeting him at The Saloon at two and then we'll take a cab back to the airport," Debra answered.

"The Saloon's just down the street," Martha said. "I'll wait while you get something to eat and then walk over with you, okay? Oh, hell, I hope you're right about Grizzard."

———————

While they talked, and Debra had a sandwich and iced tea, the restaurant emptied of its noon crowd. By the time Martha and Debra began their walk to The Saloon, the sidewalks were empty again. Martha instructed Debra to slow down and to learn to walk "like a Southerner — slowly and patiently — or else you'll just get real sick from this heat, girl. And, for God's sake, next time wear a straw hat or the sun will fry your brains."

Debra smiled at Martha's appearance: she wore a pink floral print dress on her large frame and her straw-like blonde hair poked out in all directions from under the huge hat topped with a bobbing pink rose.

It was a little after two by the time they reached the bar. It was dark and blessedly cool inside. Instead of trying to locate Bobby in the dim interior or groping her way to a table, Martha simply stood inside the door and yelled, "Bobby! Hey, boy, you here?"

A gravelly whiskey voice answered, "Not now, he ain't. That you, old girl?" A wizened old man in a baggy gray suit came ambling over to the two women. Martha caught both his hands with hers and smiled warmly. "Hey, there, Judge. It's been a long time. You still telling the youngsters how to run things?"

"Hell, no. I gave up. The whole damned world is just too ass-backwards to understand. I got a little place near here and I'm writing the history of Tallahassee. That is, when I'm not in here," the old man replied.

"You know Jay Schneider's boy, Bobby? You say he's been here?" Martha asked.

"Yup. Just like his old man. Sat here about an hour and put away about five stiff ones . . . calm as can be. Walked a straight line out of here with a girl on each arm."

"Did he say where he was going, Judge?" Martha asked.

"Nope. But I recognized one of those cuties as being a barmaid over at Studebaker's. If you find him there, thank him for me, will you? He left a fifty with the bar saying it was for me to drink on," the Judge replied.

"Thank you. Take care, okay?" Martha said as she and Debra left the bar. Standing outside in the heat again, Debra asked, "Why would Bobby just leave like that? He knows the pilot wants to take off before four."

"Come on. Let's get a cab and find Bobby, Debra. I'll tell you about him and that whole family on the way to Studebaker's," Martha answered.

There was a hotel across the street with two taxi cabs in front of it. Both looked empty until they saw the drivers slouched down in their seats asleep. Rousing one, Debra and Martha started for the bar and Martha began to explain Bobby.

"My family has known his for years. The Weils and the Schneiders go way back. There's been some mixing and mingling, too. Probably Bobby and I are third cousins or something. Anyway, my granddaddy and daddy just got tighter with money and holier-than-thou when they started rolling in money from the sale of orange groves to developers. But Bobby's granddaddy and daddy went the opposite way: they drank, and roared around the county in big cars, and made a lot of farm gals pregnant, I hear. Well, Bobby's mother was a meek little thing. It was one of those arranged marriages between big landowners. Anyway, she had three boys one right after another. The oldest one was just like his dad — real wild. He and Bobby's dad used to have some rip-roaring fights. It just about broke his mother's heart. The boy left home, enlisted, and was killed in training camp in some kind of accident. That left Bobby and his younger brother, Bradley. Bradley told everyone that he wanted to be a priest. What he didn't tell them was that he was gay, felt guilty, and was using every kind of drug he could get his hands on. A real sad little guy. He went a little crazy a few years ago. What happened has been covered up, but rumor has it that he took a knife to his daddy one night. Now no one talks about him. He's in a private institution. That leaves Bobby. Bright, pretty Bobby. Adored by his parents and given everything. What Bobby wasn't given, he took. I guess he started out nice enough, but now he's real spoiled, Debra. He's heavily into drugs, too, girl. Excuse the language, but he also fucks anything that moves. Somehow, he keeps alert enough to put together some really smart land deals, but I don't know how he does it what with the pill-popping and stuff. I don't know how long his body can take the abuse. I always liked Bobby, you know. I mean, even though I'm older, his smile could always melt me. It's sweet, you know? There's a real bright person in there — got good grades at the University and was president of the most popular fraternity on campus."

Martha stopped talking and looked cautiously at Debra. Then, deciding something, she continued talking.

"I know I drink too much. When I have a few belts I forget that I'm fat and not married. The people around me tolerate my loud talk and rowdy behavior. Hell, they'll excuse anything if your roots go far enough down into Palmetto County. But sometimes I'm not as drunk as I pretend. That night at your welcome party I hated you. All pretty and thin and bright as a new penny and so damned innocent. So I gave you a little boozy warning about the good ol' boys, remember? Maybe to scare you so you'd go back to Beverly Hills. But now it's different. You've been here four months and I've seen you work hard and I like you. I only had iced tea for lunch, so I'm sober and I'm going to tell you some things for your own good."

Debra noticed that the cab driver had leaned back to better hear their conversation as he drove.

"I don't like conversations that begin with 'for your own good,' Martha," Debra replied.

"My intentions <u>are</u> good, really. Look, it's this way: I've overheard some things. People talk freely around me because they think I won't remember anything after a few drinks. But I do, sometimes. Something is cooking with those good ol' boys, Debra. Bobby included. It has to do with the land around those donated acres they decided to call Palmetto Park. They make fun of you, Debra. Luther gets a big kick out of the time he stranded you in the swamp. Don't look so surprised, for God's sake! Yes, it was intentional. Haven't you ever wondered why those smart guys on the board of directors would hire an outsider from Beverly Hills — a woman as executive director? Haven't you ever stood outside the situation and really looked at yourself and the way it is? This ain't a Hollywood movie, kid!"

Martha looked angry. Her face was getting redder and her breathing was rapid.

"Martha, I know why they hired me. They needed someone unconnected to all the established networks. Someone the public could perceive as untainted. You know how the retirees view most of our board — as a bunch of money men just out for themselves. The public wouldn't have believed anyone from Palmetto County recommended by those fellows. I'm new," Debra replied.

There was something in what Martha was saying that was making Debra feel defensive. She felt uncomfortable because, in the past, when she had reacted defensively to something like that, it usually meant there was an element of truth involved.

"Okay, kiddo. Look, we're here at Studebaker's. Let's just go in and pull Bobby out and get him into this cab, okay? But please be careful, Debra. You might feel you're on a real roll right now because of the possibility of state funding, but believe me; you could have opened a whole can of worms by getting that money. Just be smart."

Martha told the driver to wait and she and Debra went into the turquoise and pink building constructed out of someone's dream of the 1950s. Inside, although it was three in the afternoon, revolving colored lights played throughout the interior while Little Richard screamed over the sound system.

Women dressed like carhops from the 1950s carried drinks to dim corners. Next to the empty dance floor was an old blue and white Studebaker convertible as part of the decor. Martha led the way over to a waitress leaning on the bar talking to another "carhop."

"We're looking for a blond, good-looking fellow about thirty-two," Martha said.

"Aren't we all!" the waitress replied with a laugh, and she nudged her companion.

"His name is Bobby. We're friends of his and heard he might be here." Martha insisted.

"Friends, huh? Well, if you are, you two might just be the answer. Sally and I have been trying to decide what to do with him before Joe, the manager, comes on at four. The guy you're looking for is over there." The waitress gestured to the car next to the dance floor.

Debra and Martha could see no one. They walked over to the shiny "prop" car and looked into the back seat. Bobby was asleep in the convertible while colored lights played over his angelic face.

He was not easy to rouse. Debra was anxious, knowing that Tommy would be pacing the tarmac at the airport, calculating the chances of an afternoon storm. She and Martha shook Bobby and struggled to prop him up in the back seat. Debra enlisted the nonchalant help of Sally, the waitress, to get coffee for him. She cajoled him to drink some while Martha slapped his face. Bobby finally mumbled, "In my pants pocket. Give me the pills." Martha brushed aside Debra's objections and, finding the pills, put two on his tongue. He sipped the coffee and almost gagged on the pills, but he swallowed them. Within five minutes he was alert enough to walk. Holding him upright between the two of them, Debra and Martha half-carried him to the waiting cab.

It was after four o'clock by the time they got to the airport and found Tommy next to the Cessna. Large cumulus clouds had formed spectacular white mountains in the eastern sky.

"We're not going, folks," Tommy stated calmly.

"Hey, guy, you and I have flown in skies a whole lot more threatening than this one," Bobby replied. He was alert after the cab ride and showed little evidence of his earlier stupor.

Martha stated that she would wait with them at the airport until a decision was made. Debra wasn't worried about flying in a storm; she had, in fact, flown through many storms in small private planes in California. The flight back to Palmetto County was only two hours and she wanted to leave. The day had tired her. She wanted to shorten her time with these people as much as possible. The thought of spending the night in Tallahassee worrying about Bobby's behavior was distressing, and she dismissed it as untenable.

"I'm not flying, Bobby," Tommy again stated.

Bobby walked over to Tommy and pushed his face close to the pilot's. "You are, bozo. This is no time to go candy-ass on me. You've flown in worse skies. Now you know that one word from me would end this soft job with Frank. So get smart and get moving. I want to go home — <u>now</u>."

Martha leaned toward Debra and whispered, "See? A spoiled brat."

Debra thought Bobby's behavior heavy-handed and was surprised at his shift from being Tommy's hunting buddy to his superior. But then, after what she had learned today, she realized that Bobby, and maybe others in Palmetto County, couldn't be neatly categorized as benign country characters. She wanted to go home and call Alistair. She suddenly missed his strong arms and wonderful Australian accent. She wanted to tell him about the possible funding. Strange, Bobby hadn't mentioned the probable success of their mission on the ride to the airport with Martha. She hoped his lack of enthusiasm was caused by his alcohol consumption.

Tommy's mouth was set in a hard line and his manner was stiff. "Yes, sir, Master Bobby. Whatever you want, sir. Get in and fasten those seat belts," he replied.

Debra saw Bobby momentarily consider reacting to Tommy's sarcasm but then dismiss it as he got into the plane. Again, he sat in the back. Tommy gestured to Debra to get into the copilot's seat.

With a quick, "Thank you, Martha, for everything." Debra, too, boarded.

The takeoff over the thick greenery of residential Tallahassee was smooth. Banking the plane, Tommy pointed out the sun-lit Capitol Building against the backdrop of the mountainous clouds which were deepening in color from white to gray.

"How did it go down there?" he asked over the plane's noise. Debra smiled and gave him a thumbs-up response.

"Hey, hey! That's great!" Tommy said, and then added, "And I'll bring us home successfully, too."

Soon they were flying over the Gulf, having left the land to take a more direct, southerly route. Debra could see the water change color from turquoise to slate gray as the sky darkened and the sunlight weakened. To her left she saw two snowy egrets flying against the dark clouds. She marveled at the luminescent brightness of their white bodies struck by the slanting rays of the sun setting in the west. Looking down, she saw a few pleasure boats and fishing vessels scuttling into coastline sanctuaries.

It began to get bumpy. Then, over to her left, coming from the black clouds in the east, Debra saw monstrous lightning bolts. Suddenly, the plane dropped.

"Oh, shit," Bobby exclaimed loudly from the back seat. Debra glanced at Tommy and saw him respond to Bobby's words with a small satisfied smile. He quickly leveled the plane and his intensity increased.

They were definitely in the storm now and the sensation was similar to that of a roller coaster ride Debra had experienced ten years ago. She had avoided amusement rides ever since. The noise was deafening as the plane labored through the turbulence and thunder rolled around them. It was not too loud, however, to miss hearing the agonized retching sounds from the back seat.

The odor of sickness filled the small cabin. When Debra turned to assess Bobby's condition she saw him vomiting into a crumpled newspaper which was not adequate to handle the copious result of booze, pills, and a severely disturbed metabolism. The back of the plane would never be the same again, Debra thought, as her stomach heaved slightly at the sight and odor. She didn't feel much sympathy for Bobby, and she wondered if it was her fear of the storm that cancelled her compassion or her anger toward him for insisting that they fly. Looking at him now, Debra realized that his outward arrogance hid a spoiled little boy, as Martha had said. His current vulnerable state elicited some of the sympathy she hadn't felt a moment ago. It was only a small amount of sympathy, however.

Turning her concentration back to the forward view, and ignoring Bobby's condition, was all that enabled her to avoid getting sick, too. She was frightened, though. The plane felt very fragile as the storm buffeted it. The jarring random movements of the plane caused the craft to make protesting sounds of metal under great stress. The control panel seemed brightly lit now, and the darkness outside the cabin increased Debra's sensation of being in a black bag shaken by some malevolent force.

She knew she wasn't going to die, and that certain knowledge lessened her fear. The experience, she thought, was just damned unpleasant. The fetid air in the close quarters increased Debra's growing claustrophobia. She wanted to open a door or window. She wanted cool rain on her body. She wanted out! Debra felt that nothing in Florida was what it seemed: the tropical skies turned into death traps; lazy, smiling alligators turned into man-eaters; nice country folk with little-boy names turned into menacing "rednecks," and the movie she had created in her mind about bringing culture to a tropical paradise was turning into a real-life satire with herself as the bumbling, naive fool.

Tommy was working hard. His face was grim and his body rigid. Debra concentrated on his determined, efficient manner to quell her internal litany of depressing thoughts.

Suddenly the sky was light and a strange sensation of smoothness took hold of the plane's occupants. They were out of it. Rain clouds scurried around them, but the plane sought and found calm air. In the quiet Debra could hear her rapid breathing. She realized her jaw hurt and, as she relaxed it, she knew that she had been clenching her teeth the whole time.

She looked at Tommy and saw lines of sweat running down the side of his face and neck. His shirt was completely wet. She dreaded what she would see when she turned to look at Bobby. Her dread was well-founded: he looked dead. There was no color in his face and he was slumped sideways, passed out. His clothes were matted and soaked with vomit.

For the first time in what seemed like hours to Debra, Tommy spoke. "Well, goddamn. That was a real pant-pisser. Everyone okay?" He glanced over at Debra. She smiled and nodded but gestured to the back seat and shook her head. As the plane approached the small airport, Debra could see the storm front moving farther out into the Gulf, leaving Palmetto County glistening green below. The runway was slick from the recent downpour and the plane bounced twice and skidded when they landed. Bobby groaned at the first bump; the sound reassured Debra that he wasn't unconscious.

She saw Johnny running toward the plane from the Quonset hut. His solid athlete's body was barreling through deep puddles and causing huge splashes in his eagerness to reach them. Tommy quickly cut the engine and jumped from the plane as Johnny yanked open the passenger door. His boyish face reflected concern and anger as he grabbed Debra and lifted her from the plane. As soon as he put her on the ground he whirled to confront Tommy.

"You idiot! You goddamn idiot!" Johnny yelled. He took hold of Tommy under both arms, picked him up, and started shaking him. Tommy, at five foot ten and 140 pounds, was no match for the athlete's six foot four and 220 pounds of muscle. The pilot went limp and looked resigned as Johnny continued to yell, "Idiot!" and shake him.

Debra felt a strange sense of languor and found that her legs and arms would not move quickly on command. She slowly tapped Johnny's back and repeated, "It's not his fault, Johnny. It's not his fault."

Finally, Johnny put the limp pilot back on the ground and turned to look questioningly at Debra. She gestured into the plane and said, "Bobby insisted. He threatened Tommy, saying he'd make sure he'd lose his job if he refused to fly us. Tommy got us through hell, but we wouldn't have been there except for Bobby . . . and me. I didn't protest. I didn't know what a summer storm in Florida meant. I'm sorry." Debra's tongue felt thick and her words were slowly paced. She was very tired.

Johnny put one arm around her as support and dragged her along with him the few feet back to the plane. He looked through the open door into the back seat and exclaimed, "Good God. What is that stinking thing in there? Is it human?"

"Cut the jokes, man. I think I almost died. I can't move out of this mess." Bobby's feeble voice wafted out from the back seat along with the strong odor.

Johnny half-carried, half-dragged Debra over to Tommy and said, "Get her into the building. I'll get Bobby out."

Tommy and Debra turned gratefully from the plane and, with their arms linked and supporting each other, they walked slowly over to the small building.

Dear, sweet Johnny, Debra thought. He must have called Betty Lou at the office to find out their arrival time and had been here waiting for them during the storm. There really are some nice people in this place, Debra thought. She was eager to tell him and the other members of the board of directors about Senator Grizzard's response. Right now, though, she wanted a drink, a very necessary shower, and to lie on her bed under the cooling breeze of the ceiling fan.

�֎ ✤ ✤

Chapter Ten

They finished unloading Johnny's four-wheel drive truck and, slinging the shovels, stakes, and coiled rope over their shoulders, marched toward the low swampy area of the park site. It was Betty Lou who started chanting, "Left, right, left, right."

Everyone, even Aunt Alice, who was walking slowly behind them carrying only a sun parasol, joined in. They were giddy with happiness, camaraderie and the hot June sun. That morning Debra had received the awaited telephone call from Senator Grizzard. They had the grant: both the House and the Senate had approved it, and the Governor would sign it.

After excited telephone calls, the volunteer work crew was assembled: Johnny, William, Alice, and Michael, an architect from Tampa, joined Betty Lou and Debra on the site. Johnny had introduced Michael, thirtyish, bespectacled, and soft-spoken, to Debra about a month ago. Michael wanted his firm to be known in the region and, after listening to Debra and Johnny explain the park project, donated the design of the Nature Center. Debra had immediately informed the newspaper of his generous donation of time and talent. A couple of weeks ago, with typical optimism, he and Debra had staked the building site which was on slightly elevated land. Today, with the added volunteers, they would stake the length of the nature boardwalk, some of it through swampy areas. But this day was different: they knew that the Nature Center would be built.

Debra looked at her "work crew" and smiled; all of them, including her, looked like "Florida Crackers" in their jeans, boots, straw hats, long sleeved cotton shirts, and neck bandanas to catch the sweat. They planned to do as much as possible in the 90 degree heat before the inevitable afternoon rains began. She looked at Johnny and Michael, in the lead, talking animatedly, and was grateful that they had left their offices on a work day to help her. William was usually available to help with work on the park site, but today he would be mostly busy watching over Alice. Both the young men had even brought hip-high wading boots with shoulder straps in case the marsh water was deep; these wading rigs were thrown over their shoulders as they walked to the designated area. Debra enjoyed looking at Johnny. She marveled at his brawn: it looked as if he could pound a stake into the ground with just his fist. Alice's voice spoke softly behind her, "Lordy, Lordy. I do want to be with you children on this happy day, but if dear William will just find me a shady, dry spot to rest, I think I can help the most by staying out of your way. I'll shout encouragement, though, child!"

The thought of Alice shouting anything was incongruous to Debra. Her soft, feminine presence was barely felt or acknowledged at the board meetings, which struck Debra as strange since it was her late husband who had accumulated the thousands of acres of which Palmetto Park was a part. She had become Debra's friend during her daily telephone calls to the project's office, "just to see how you are, dear." Debra knew that Alice supported the park project, even though she often referred to it as "Luther's Scheme Dream." The ninety-two-year-old woman's fey comments often startled Debra, and once, during one of Alice's daily calls, she had asked her what she meant at the welcome party when she stated, "Pay no attention to the Mad Hatter." Alice simply laughed softly and didn't answer.

William's fondness for the old woman, and hers for him, was obvious as he gently settled her on a blanket under a nearby oak tree and brought her a can of iced tea from the cooler. He told the others to wait for him; he didn't like the idea of them going into the brush without him.

"Snakes, you know. I wore this side arm for a reason."

Not even the possibility of snakes could dampen Debra's euphoria as she and the others waited for William. The land appeared benign and beautiful to her.

"You did it, Debra! It's just beginning to really sink in. Wait'll those 'naysayers' on the board find out! Wait'll the newspaper hits the streets tomorrow! Oh, boy!" Betty Lou's sweet, plain face was flushed with pleasure.

"We did it. Your nimble fingers typed up a smashing proposal and your enthusiasm kept me going, friend," Debra replied as she gave Betty Lou a quick hug.

"Don't we get one, too, lady?" Michael asked with a grin. "Johnny here — and I — well, we've been morale boosters, too, haven't we?"

"More than that. And you two know it. But you'll get hugs when the last stake is in." Turning to Johnny, she said, for the third time that day, "Do you realize that, with the money coming here by September fifteenth we can start construction on the building before October fifteenth and beat that deed restriction Stanley keeps mentioning?"

"Yes, Debra, yes. We know, we know. I've said it before; this park became a reality the minute you stepped off that plane in Tampa." His boyish face was dimpled in an exuberant smile, and Debra felt her heart flip a little at his kindness.

With William leading the way, they left Alice humming to herself under the tree. Single file, they carefully walked through chest-high grass to the "base camp," a clear area at the beginning of the projected boardwalk system. Betty Lou and Debra spread out the site plans and anchored them with stones. They put the extra stakes, and the equipment that wouldn't be used for the men's first foray into the marsh, in neat stacks. The men planned to wade out into the wetlands southward and return to the base as they needed more stakes. William, after again warning Johnny and Michael about snakes, returned to stay with Alice.

The two women laughed at the men as they struggled to get into their hip-high wading boots and then, awkwardly, stomped off into the marsh weighted down with stakes and coils of rope. The high brush immediately hid them. Five minutes passed before the women heard an unintelligible shout coming from the waders' direction and then raucous laughter.

"What is it? What happened?" Debra shouted.

"It's Johnny. He's sinking!" Michael yelled back.

Debra turned, startled, to Betty Lou and said, "Let's go in."

"If they're laughing, he's safe, Debra."

"I want to make sure." The thought of sweet Johnny being in trouble upset her, and she wondered why she thought of that strong young man as vulnerable. She walked quickly into the weeds at the place the men had entered and was soon surrounded by prickly tall grass. Fortunately, the ground was only slightly soggy and her boots were adequate protection. She heard Betty Lou's resigned, "Oh, well, here goes," as her assistant followed.

By seeing where the tall grass was broken or bent, Debra was able to proceed along the men's path and toward their voices. Suddenly, she stumbled up against Michael's back, and Betty Lou walked into her. Michael had braced himself by digging in his heels, but the impact of the two women nearly threw him off balance.

"Shit," he said, and then, laughing, he added, "The cavalry arrived, Johnny. Now you're saved."

The women had to peer around Michael to see that he was strenuously pulling on a rope with which he had managed to lasso the larger man who was in deep, swampy terrain. Johnny was almost up to his hips in muck with muddy water beginning to rush over the top of his hip-high wading boots. He was simply too heavy for the wetter areas and getting heavier by the minute. The hip waders had sealed his fate.

Seeing his consternation, Debra began to laugh. Soon, all three of the "rescuers" were helpless with laughter, holding each other as tears rolled down their cheeks and their stomachs ached. Johnny, meanwhile, was patiently, laboriously, struggling to get out of his waders by twisting sideways and down toward the water while tugging at his boots. Bootless, finally, he lunged almost horizontally at Michael on the higher ground, hoping to be pulled to safety. Michael, however, was not prepared for the lunge, and, before Debra could try to brace Michael, he was in the shallower mud with Johnny. Beyond the two men were the abandoned hip-high waders with just the tops visible, looking like half of a cut-off man.

Betty Lou's and Debra's laughter stopped suddenly but then, realizing Michael could easily maneuver in his waders and help Johnny, they became convulsed with it again.

It was a motley-looking crew that made its way back to Alice and William under the tree. The two men tried to maintain their dignity before William and explained that they had come back for some iced tea before tackling the swamp again. William, with a twinkle in his eyes, said he thought a "work break" was a good idea. "Besides," he added, "I want to show

Debra something. Why don't you all stay here with Miss Alice, while I take the 'boss woman' on a short walk."

Debra longed for a cool drink, but something about William's attitude compelled her to follow him as he walked away from the group toward the site of the Nature Center. His silent walk through the thick vegetation reminded Debra of her father's admonition on one of their camping trips when she was a child, *Walk like an Indian, honey*. However, her father never wore a gun.

William, without turning his head, said quietly, "Don't worry, miss, if all the stakes don't get in today. They will. I've known Johnny since he was a little kid, and he's good for his word. Persistent, too."

They came to the site that they had staked previously, and Debra was struck by the mounds of sandy fill that surrounded it and covered some nearby trees halfway up their trunks. There had always been some fill, excess from the preliminary road work, near the site of the future Nature Center, but nothing compared to what now surrounded it.

William stopped, pointed to the trees, and said, "They're killing them, miss."

"Who, or what, is killing them, William?"

"The fill is smothering the tree roots. Why is all this fill being dumped here? And why aren't those fellows on your board, who know it'll bring in money for the park, carting it off and selling it? Something else, miss. Look how close to the Nature Center the road is being built! Just don't make no sense, if you ask me."

Debra didn't respond immediately. She walked around the site and looked at all the trees slowly dying. She then walked off the staked site and climbed a mound of fill to see a wide park road, fully graded, just fifty feet away.

Returning to where William stood, she said, "I don't understand it, William. The site plans show the park road to be much farther away from the Nature Center. Bobby and Jim have been supervising the road building. They certainly seem to know what they're doing. They've been pleased that donations have enabled us to do the roadwork."

William shook his head slowly. "Some of these trees have been here a real long time. You told me that you picked this site for the Nature Center because you wanted the people to see these trees. Someone better tell those fellows that the fill has to be moved." She touched his arm and said, "I'll tell them, William. Thank you for showing me. I didn't know that fill could kill trees. And I'll find out about the road, too. But it looks like it's going to have to stay there. Maybe we'll have to move the Nature Center site."

When they returned to Alice's "outdoor salon," they found her talking to Betty Lou. The men had returned to their staking work, after Johnny stated he'd stay on higher ground.

Betty Lou was obviously fascinated by Alice and turned eagerly to Debra.

"Debra! Did you know that this park is on an ancient holy site of the Seminole Indians?"

When Debra responded that she hadn't known, Alice said, "Oh, yes, dear. Why William and I often feel their vibrations when we're on the land! Isn't that right, William?"

"Yes, ma'am," he replied softly.

"And I've told both Luther and William that I hear their chants sometimes at night. In fact, just last week I told Luther that we had to build a temple here. A beautiful temple to their gods and to our God. A true joining of cultures and beliefs. A true Floridian blend. A final reconciliation after so much bloodshed!"

"What did Brother Luther say to that, ma'am?" William asked, just as Debra was about to ask the same question.

"The dear boy doesn't understand the importance of some things. But I must say I was surprised at his brusque reply that no one was going to build anything on the site except him! I thought the board, including me, decided those things." Alice shook her head slowly and added, "Marcus would have listened to me, isn't that right, William?"

"Yes, ma'am, he surely would have." Turning to Debra with a faint question in his eyes, he said softly, "Miss, Luther is a good man, but it seems to me someone ought to talk to him about a few things. I'm going to take Miss Alice back to the ranch now. Why don't you and Betty Lou take some of this canned iced tea to your friends? Just watch your step real careful-like going there. I'll come back to you after I get her settled."

Debra thanked Alice for her "moral support" during the boardwalk staking and gathered a few cans of still-cold iced tea for the work crew. Walking back to the clearing with Betty Lou, she was quiet, thinking about what Alice had said and what William had shown her.

Betty Lou said, solicitously, "The heat's too much. You're looking a bit done-in. Why, you should be somewhere cool celebrating the grant! And with some 'cool' guy, too, if I may be presumptuous."

Debra answered with a laugh. She briefly wondered what Betty Lou would think of her if she knew about her arrangement with Alistair. She dismissed him from her thoughts and thought again about Alice's and William's conversations. By the time they reached the clearing, her skin felt prickly and a heavy uneasiness had fallen over her.

Large, threatening clouds were piling up on the horizon preparing to unload their afternoon rain.

Chapter Eleven

Harvey couldn't believe it. The president of Palmetto Community College sat absolutely still and stared at the brass antique clock on his desk. It was 9:45 on a beautiful June morning and he felt betrayed. Suddenly, his hand that held the telephone began to tremble.

He found his voice and yelled into the telephone, "You're either lying or crazy! Or maybe this is your idea of a joke? What the hell is going on?"

He listened and felt the sweat bead on his forehead.

"We got half of what we asked for, fifty thousand dollars, and she got five hundred thousand dollars? What happened? Why didn't you get to Grizzard and Goodell first? Make fun of the proposal? You promised me that you'd make Tallahassee rough for her, remember?"

He stood up with the phone in his hand, and listened impatiently to the voice at the other end.

"You mean to tell me that just because Grizzard said it was a 'damn good proposal,' that woman waltzed away with state money? Things don't happen that way in Tallahassee! I've been working on those legislators for years and they only throw crumbs to us! She, or someone, did something to those boys to get that kind of money. You get more information. I'll call you later."

He slammed down the telephone, walked to the middle of his office, and yelled through the closed door, "Get in here, Nancy!"

When she walked quickly into the office, her frightened face was drained of the animation that usually passed for prettiness.

"I want you to get Luther on the phone. His uncle donated the land for this college and this college was just betrayed! Cheated out of money by a woman representing a park on land that is also from the Bradenburgs."

Nancy knew that he was talking aloud to himself; she was just supposed to stand there quietly.

"Why Luther ever decided to build a park is beyond me," he continued, "why not give the land to the college? We need more land! Our friends in Tallahassee said they would stop her. They didn't. Now they say, as an excuse, that the money she's getting is from a different state source than the one we applied to. As if that matters! The legislators wouldn't give both of us money, even if the funds were from different sources! They figured 'just so much for Palmetto County and no more.' And she, that 'flimflam lady,' got the lion's share! I ask you, is that justice?"

Nancy, taking her cue, replied meekly, "No, sir."

"Get that old buzzard on the phone."

As Nancy turned to leave, she almost collided with Luther. Blushing, she hurried through the door.

"I gather you mean me," he said to Harvey, who looked momentarily stricken.

Harvey recovered quickly and mumbled, "Hello, Luther." before striding back to his desk chair and sitting down heavily.

"I'm upset. I apologize for my outburst. You won't believe what I just heard. It's shocked me," he said.

Luther sat in the chair facing Harvey and said, "You mean about Palmetto Park receiving five hundred thousand dollars to build a Nature Center? My dear fellow, I've known about it since eight this morning. That little gal is full of surprises, isn't she? We agreed to the fund-raising trip up there, never dreaming she'd succeed. Why, I was all set to have her over to the ranch this evening for a condolence drink after the state budget was announced. If I wasn't so angry I'd be laughing at all of us right now."

"You're angry? Why?" Harvey asked, surprised.

"Where have you been, man? Surely you've gathered that I'm not eager to see the park rapidly developed! I'm here to tell you that I, too, think the college should have the money you asked for this year, not the Palmetto Park project. Perhaps you know ways to get a grant rescinded after the Governor has signed the budget?"

"Maybe. But first, I'll admit I'm confused. You've always dropped hints about not wanting the project to succeed, but I've never known why. Would you rather see it used for education rather than for cultural uses? If so, why didn't you just donate it to the college?"

"Let's just slow down a bit. First of all, I don't want 'watchdogs' from the Department of Parks and Recreation hanging around, and, believe me, they will with five hundred thousand dollars of state money being used." Blood rushed to Luther's lined face as he became agitated thinking about the grant. When he continued it was as if he was speaking to himself: "Damn it all, anyway! It's a sweet deal I've set up with Ed Haze, and I won't have it blown out of the water by a 'do-good' female. After October fifteenth, with no construction begun on the land, the park goes to the Department of Agriculture.

I'll buy it back for a nominal fee at a public auction. And for the last five years I've received a tax break for the donation."

"So this 'extension' Stanley keeps talking about is a lie? Just to slow down Debra?" Harvey asked.

"That's right. Didn't work, obviously. With the state money she'll begin construction before the deadline. Well, we can't let it happen. Do you know how much that land will be worth once the bypass is in place? A considerable sum, my man. You probably know that Jim, and Bobby, and maybe even Rufus and Stanley, are buying land around the park site. The grapevine works well in our community."

"No, I didn't. Apparently I haven't known very much. But it's a relief to know that the land isn't going to be used for nonessential activities. I'm pleased that it will be back in the hands of a Bradenburg. Don't worry. I'll call some people in Tallahassee. We'll figure out a way to get the grant rescinded."

"You do that. And, in a week or so, after you see if you can pull a few strings up there, I'll get the boys together at the ranch to talk about this little surprise we got today. Meanwhile, we'll all act very happy and congratulate the little lady. Now, I'd be very pleased if you'd forget everything I said today. I got a little carried away." Luther uncoiled his lanky body from the chair and prepared to leave.

Harvey quickly left his chair and walked around his ornate desk to Luther. "Why don't you and I meet a little earlier at your ranch? Before the 'boys' get there? I think we should discuss, privately, our plans for the park land," Harvey suggested with a confident smile. He was sure now that he could convince Luther to give the land to the college, particularly since he, Harvey, had "privileged information" to use as leverage.

Nancy heard everything. In her embarrassed rush past Luther she hadn't closed the office door. At first, sitting at her desk outside Harvey's office, she didn't understand why the men were so upset. And she really didn't care. She disliked Harvey Brown. When he was foiled in some endeavor she was glad, except when he took his frustration out on her. He was an unpleasant and arrogant man, and he treated the college staff terribly. There were stories around campus about him; rumors circulated regarding his "fondness" for college students, both male and female. Nancy's predecessor once considered filing a sexual harassment suit against him, but abandoned the idea when she realized no one in the outside community would believe her. Harvey Brown was respected and liked by the powerful "good ol' boys."

Nancy, at one point during Luther's and Harvey's conversation, went to the door to close it. She didn't when she realized what she was hearing: the Palmetto Park project was a hoax and Debra didn't know it. Tommy, Nancy's boyfriend, often talked about Debra, saying how nice she was and how brave she had been when they hit bad weather coming back from Tallahassee.

Nancy listened to them talk, and, although she didn't understand everything, she heard enough to be angry and a little frightened. When she heard Luther preparing to leave, she walked quickly to the file cabinet which was on the other side of the room, pulled open a drawer, and began to shuffle the papers.

Luther and Harvey said their congenial goodbyes in the outer office without even noticing her. When Harvey returned to his office and shut the door, Nancy closed the file drawer with a loud slam.

They didn't even notice me! I'm such a 'non-person' to them that they didn't even care if I heard them! she realized. Nancy wondered what Tommy would say when she told him what she'd heard. Five o'clock seemed a long time away to her.

※ ※ ※

Chapter Twelve

A tall, hefty female in cutoff jeans and a dirty plaid shirt was waiting at the ranch entrance when Harvey arrived. When he drove up to the long wooden gate she looked at him intently and then unlocked the padlock. Effortlessly, she swung open the gate to let him drive onto the ranch road. As soon as he was inside, she walked the gate back into position and locked it.

She looked familiar to Harvey. Her name was "Sara" or "Sally," he thought. He could never keep Luther's strange, silent ranch hands separate in his mind; it didn't matter how many times he saw them during visits to the ranch. He often wondered what they did besides security work. Of course, there were the cattle to herd or whatever they did to them, he thought.

As he drove along the winding dirt road to the ranch house, he marveled anew at the lushness of Luther's land. A sharp pang of envy hit him. *What a lucky bastard. Imagine inheriting all of this. He never had to struggle or scheme*, he thought with bitterness. Harvey's envy attacks were frequent. He couldn't even enjoy the beauty of nature without wanting to own it.

He slowed down as a golf cart appeared on the road ahead of him. A handsome young man, stripped to the waist, drove the cart past him and acknowledged his presence with a solemn nod. Harvey experienced acute avarice and fantasized the rest of the way to the ranch house; he imagined all the marvelous things the ranch hands did together on their time off from work.

Seeing Luther waiting for him at the door brought him back to reality. He needed to think clearly if he wanted to use this time alone with Luther productively.

"Good afternoon, Mr. President," Luther said jovially as Harvey left his car and walked up the steps to the entrance. "Come on in, away from this merciless sun which, by the way, is over the 'yardarm,' as sailors say. Meaning, my friend, that it wouldn't be improper to have a little branch water and bourbon."

Harvey followed Luther into the dark, warm interior of the cavernous house, thinking for the hundredth time how he would decorate the place if he had Luther's money. *Decorate, hell*, he thought. *I'd tear the place down and start over.*

Aloud to Luther he said, "None for me, thanks. Iced tea would be welcome, though, if you have it."

To Harvey's relief they walked through the gloomy living room and onto the long screened porch that ran the length of the house. It was a mess, as usual, filled with old lawn furniture. Harvey saw torn pieces of paper and old clothing which gave evidence of the raccoon's presence, and he glanced quickly around the porch to see if the animal was in residence.

"Don't worry. Aunt Alice has Rumpus with her in her wing of the house. Neither will disturb us. Pick a chair, I'll get our drinks," Luther said as he left the porch.

Harvey found a chair that appeared relatively clean and that was in a good position to catch the late afternoon breezes. He only sat momentarily, however. The large cage that had dominated the porch for the last four months drew his attention. On his previous visits it had seemed empty; now he detected something on its floor. He walked over to it and then drew back in disgust. A large snake was sleeping in it.

Hearing Luther approach with the drinks, Harvey turned to him and said, "Why on earth are you keeping that ugly thing?"

"Did you notice how fat she is? William says she's going to be a mother. Ever see a snake have young?" When Harvey shook his head without speaking, Luther continued, "Me neither. Thought I'd keep her here until it happens. Of course, William thinks I'm daft. Here's your drink. Let's sit down and talk some before the others arrive."

Harvey took the iced tea and said, "We may as well get right to it. I know you're waiting to hear what my allies in Tallahassee say about the Palmetto Park grant. Guess you could say the news is 'mixed.'"

"'Mixed?' How?"

"Well, it seems that the grant is secure. Senator Grizzard did some heavy campaigning for it. But here's the interesting part: although the proposal is well-written and can stand on its own merits, my sources tell me that the reason the money was granted has more to do with the force of Debra's talent and sincerity. Grizzard, and Goodell, too, believe in her ability to manage the money. If Debra wasn't executive director, there's a possibility that the grant would be in jeopardy."

"Interesting. Well, from what I can gather, she isn't about to leave. Hell, some of our board and all of Palmetto County are patting her on the back because of the grant. She feels real good right now." Luther took a long swallow of bourbon, stretched out his legs, and stared out past the screened porch to the lake before turning his attention to the other man. Harvey didn't say anything; he knew Luther had something more to say.

"I'm going to be real frank with you, Harvey, and fill you in on some things. Ever hear about something called the Antilles Development Corporation? No? Well, I'm not surprised. You tend to sit in your 'ivory tower' a lot. Since the company isn't a well-kept secret anymore, you might as well learn about it. As I've said before, some of the boys have been buying land around the park site. They've been buying it through Antilles Development, an investment corporation based in the Caribbean and very reluctant to expose who its investors are. A while back, Jim approached me and asked if I wanted to put some of my money in a tax-safe, offshore investment company. It appealed to me. The boys and I like the idea that we can buy land without the public knowing about it." Pausing to sip his drink, he continued, "And, shoot, Uncle Marcus owned most of Palmetto County at one time and, even though I've just been selling bits and pieces of it, the money has accumulated. So now I have some money in the trust with Rufus' bank and some in the Caribbean. Before too long, there's going to be a lot more money."

Luther ended, what for him was a lengthy speech and turned his attention back to his lake. Harvey wondered how to bring the conversation around to his desire to have the park land for the college. He didn't care about a business deal in the Caribbean.

"Palmetto Park, Harvey, is going to be a regional shopping center surrounded by up-scale subdivisions. ADC is going to develop it after I get it back from Ed Haze. Didn't you ever wonder about my deal with him?" Harvey just shrugged his shoulders in response; he was still digesting the words, "regional shopping center."

"Well, I'll tell you anyway. You see, Ed owes me a lot. My campaign contributions, and those of fellow ranchers I arm-twisted a bit, have kept old Ed in office a mighty long time. Once I figured out what I wanted, I 'pulled the string': I donated the land to the Department of Agriculture, got a tax write-off, and then set up a nonprofit organization with Bobby as president. Since, by agreement, the Department didn't want the land, when Bobby asked for the land for a cultural center, the Department deeded it over to the Palmetto Park project. And that's where that little ol' deed restriction comes in. When October fifteenth arrives, the land reverts to the Department, an 'auction' is held, and I get it back. Or, rather, ADC gets it. Bobby, Jim and I have planned this carefully. When the shopping center is developed, this ranch land right next to it is going to skyrocket in value, as will all the surrounding land. And we all know that the bypass our dear Debra touted so well in Tallahassee will increase the land value also. The shopping center and the subdivisions will be right next to a major north-south freeway!" Luther began to chuckle and patted Harvey's knee.

"I'm appalled, Luther," Harvey said.

"Appalled? You should be applauding! Think of all those pretty new students who will be moving into this area! Think of how your college will grow! Oh, I almost forgot another thing our Debra did. She got our shopping mall roads constructed! Free from our community!" Luther doubled up in glee.

Harvey felt as if the ground was shifting under him. His palms began to sweat and his mind began to quickly devise strategies. The realization that everyone except him was going to get something struck him with a physical pain in his stomach. A silent scream, *It's not fair!* shook him. Harvey knew that he had survived worse power plays than this. All he had to do was clear his mind. Something would come to him. It did, and Harvey exhaled a deep sigh.

"How clever of you, Luther. It obviously pleases you to realize how you've fooled so many of Palmetto's citizens. I wonder how they would react if they knew. Your late uncle would have been surprised, too. He had such grand plans for this county." Harvey sipped his iced tea and saw that Luther was looking at him warily.

"I completely support your desire to remove Debra, and I'm sure that when the others arrive we can plan a strategy to do so, but, to be blunt, what's in it for me? Granted, it would be nice to have a competitor for state funds leave my territory, but that's not quite enough. Do you remember that several years ago you told me that your uncle purchased the mineral rights when he bought land? I think it would be a splendid gift to the college if you donated the mineral rights from all the Bradenburg land to our endowment fund. You'd get another tax write-off and the college would receive money in one of two ways: land no one wanted could be mined for sand and possible minerals, and the mineral rights on land which people wanted could be sold to them since no one wants someone else to own what's underneath a potential subdivision."

Luther laughed and, to Harvey's annoyance, patted Harvey's knee again.

"I always said you were a smart man! If you can't get the land, you'll take what's under it. Only problem is, I don't need another tax break. Also, something as visible as a major donation to a college's endowment fund has to be handled properly by the Bradenburg Trust. I've always given Rufus his say on how the trust fund is operated. Why don't the two of you talk?"

Harvey was trying to think of a response when he heard the front door open and the men arrive. Quickly he said, "You'll understand if I'm not too enthusiastic at present about your scheme. Actually, I think your plans are a bit extreme."

"My plans? Why, Harvey, you've been right there on the board of directors and on the selection committee for the executive director! I'll have Rufus talk to you, old friend."

———•———

The strategy session lasted two hours. After Bobby, Jim, Rufus and Stanley had drinks in their hands, Luther told them what Harvey had learned from his Tallahassee contacts. The men understood that with Debra gone the state would be reluctant to release funds to an organization without a chief executive officer. They all agreed that she should leave as soon as possible.

Then Stanley said, "There's a major problem: the community totally supports her. The board of directors has no grounds to fire her, particularly after this grant from the state. If we try to trump up something, we could bring irate citizens down on us. I can just imagine Joe Casey mobilizing his 'Gray Panthers.'"

"She must be vulnerable on some point. Everyone is. Who's she dating?" Rufus asked.

"She isn't seen anywhere at night, alone or otherwise," Bobby said, "but I've heard some comments that there is someone. Maybe it's just wishful thinking on some men's part; no one likes to think that someone who looks like that is going to waste."

"If there is someone, find him. Follow her if necessary. Maybe if she has a 'friend,' he can be convinced it's to her, and his, best interests for her to resign," Luther stated, and then added, "By the way, she's a good kid and I know none of us wants this to get messy."

"Messy, huh? Seems to me that stranding her in the swamp wasn't exactly 'good clean fun,'" Rufus chuckled. "And that snake on her doorstep was a nice touch, too."

"I had nothing to do with the snake!" Luther protested

"Sure, sure," Jim said. "Look, fellows, snakes and swamps and slashed tires haven't dimmed her enthusiasm for this place or this project. I say we apply constant harassment, and I have an idea ..."

He was interrupted by Harvey, who suddenly stood, looked at his watch and said, "I have an appointment with a major donor to the college endowment fund. Sorry, I have to leave. Luther, I'm not sure I can get behind all this one hundred percent."

"I understand. We'll talk later. Good evening," Luther replied. As soon as Harvey left the porch, Luther turned to Rufus and said, "He wants his share. He wants the mineral rights to Bradenburg land. Meet with him, Rufus, negotiate a little."

"As I was saying, I have an idea," Jim continued. "She's started to do public service announcements asking for contributions. The cable station has videotaped seven of them as a donation to the project. Every time you turn on the local station, there she is, looking damned sincere and sexy. I'm sure lots of the local boys are drooling over her TV image. Her telephone number is in the book. Why not try a few weeks of obscene phone calls?"

"I bet you'd be real good at that, Jimbo," Bobby laughed.

"Not me, you ass. Just some infatuated viewer I might know," he replied.

"I don't think I want to hear anymore. As a matter of fact, I'm becoming very uncomfortable with this talk. As your legal advisor, I'm warning you that we are on dangerous ground here," Stanley said.

"No need to worry, Counselor," Luther answered, "we're just 'shooting the breeze' here. We want her to leave on her own free will, with as little fuss as possible. So why don't we just do what we've been doing, what lots of boards of directors do? Why don't we just stall on every decision, every minor detail having to do with the park, every request she makes to us? We've been doing that all along; now we'll really dig in our heels. The poor little gal won't be able to get anything done! And we'll give her a healthy severance paycheck when she decides the project isn't worth the trouble."

"I'm not too uncomfortable with that plan," Stanley responded.

"Good. That's settled then. Drink up, boys. This meeting is adjourned," Luther said, smiling.

It was deep twilight when most of the men left the ranch house. Jim stayed on the porch with Luther, finishing the bottle of bourbon in companionable silence. The two men listened as the night sounds of the frogs and crickets began.

After a while, Luther said, "You know, I really love this land. Some of my happiest times are spent just poking around on it. When this ranch goes, and the park land, it's going to be the end of the 'old' Florida in this county. Why, Seminole Indians camped under these live oaks."

"You've been listening to Alice too much. You aren't getting cold feet about our plans for this land, are you?" Jim asked.

"No, I'm sorry to say that money and power excite me. You know, until a few years ago, I always thought of the land as my uncle's. Even after he died it didn't seem to belong to me. I hated to be stuck here with Aunt Alice and resented the responsibility of the land and those damned cattle. I don't know when I started liking the place. It just happened. Sometimes I realize that I'm an old man and I wonder where I'm going to be when I die. Take my foreman, for instance. Old William doesn't own this land legally, but he does emotionally. Why, he's even picked out a place on the land where he wants his ashes scattered. Oh, hell. Sometimes I look at him and I wonder what he'd say if he knew his special spot was going to be part of a parking lot."

"We have to move this project along faster, Luther. These delays are making you a little crazy," Jim responded.

"You're right. We're sitting on a 'gold mine' and it's making us jumpy."

"Debra is making us 'jumpy,' as you say. I know people in Miami that deal quickly with situations like this."

"Too bad we aren't in Miami, then. It would make things easier for us. Here, we just sit listening to the frogs and contemplating the end of an era."

PART 3

Chapter Thirteen

The sky was blood red from the sunrise, and Debra noticed that the brackish canal water had a soft pink sheen to it. The water looked too gentle to be the home of alligators.

Everything was very quiet; not even the birds were singing. Instead of the beginning of a new day, it felt like the end of something to Debra. She sat on the dock's bench and stared at the morning paper. It announced that it was August 16, 1984, and that Betty Lou Anderson, administrative assistant to Debra Price, executive director of Palmetto Park, was in critical condition following a car accident.

Debra hadn't slept since returning from the hospital. Alistair, protesting, left after bringing her home. At five a.m. she dressed and retrieved the newspaper from her front lawn. Not wanting to go back inside, she had walked to the dock and now sat there on the bench reading, again, about Betty Lou. Her mind kept sliding away from it and juxtaposed irrelevant questions: where were the ducks? And why was the humidity oppressive so early?

She willed herself to concentrate on what had happened and what she must do. She had to call for a taxi and go to the hospital before Betty Lou was transferred to the burn unit.

A footstep made the wood dock vibrate. Debra looked up, startled, and saw Johnny standing near her. Something in his expression made her want to cry. She rose from the bench and walked into his arms sobbing. She knew what he was going to say even before he said, "Betty Lou died an hour ago."

He smoothed her hair gently as she cried on his chest. When most of her tears stopped, she raised her face to look into his eyes. Then, to her profound surprise, she pulled on his head to lower it to hers and kissed him. The feelings her action evoked made them both tremble. Their kisses were soothing, yet passionate and, to Debra, a defiant protest against death. She wanted to affirm life by melting into his vital presence.

Abruptly, however, she broke from their embrace, shocked and embarrassed by her response to his announcement. To her shame, she added to her inappropriate behavior by saying, with a shaky laugh, "Do you suppose that after all these months of drinking it, I'm weeping iced-tea tears?"

Johnny didn't respond. When she dared to look at him, she saw an infinitely compassionate look on his face.

"She never suffered. She was in a coma since the accident. I've told the hospital that we'll make the funeral arrangements this afternoon. Sit down, Debra. I need to tell you a couple of things. First of all, I love you. I won't mention it again, or what just happened between us, until you let me know you're ready to discuss it. Also, William called me at the hospital this morning, just before Betty Lou died. He was calling from his trailer but was going back to the park site where, apparently, he spent the night. He wants us to meet him there as soon as possible."

"Whatever for?" Debra asked, relieved that he had kindly, and in a matter-of-fact way, eased her embarrassment. She filed away the "I love you" until she could deal with it rationally.

"He sounded a little incoherent. He said that the park was producing 'evil' and that he had something to show us."

They drove into the park on the road that passed near the Nature Center site. After they parked at the north end of the park, they walked along a dirt path to where William told Johnny he'd be waiting. The early morning sun was quickly evaporating the dew from the glistening ferns and palmetto fronds. It caused a humid haze to blanket the low-lying vegetation and blur all of nature's sharp edges. Debra, at first, thought her vision was distorted.

How Betty Lou loved this park! she thought. It was impossible to imagine her dead. By the time they reached William, leaning against one of his favorite trees, Debra's vision was blurred by tears.

William walked unsteadily over to them. "I have a hunch, Miss Debra, that you're going to tell me that your nice friend is gone, that so?"

"Yes, William."

"I'm real sorry, but I'm not surprised. The good spirits are in danger here. Something evil is on this land," William said earnestly to Johnny and Debra.

Both of them looked at the blanket under the tree where William had spent the night. An empty bottle of whiskey was on it.

"Yup, I've been drinking. It stops the pain in my heart and it helps me to talk to the old spirits around here. We had a lot of talking to do last night. They told me to get you two here and show you what put a knife into my heart. Come. Be real quiet, though."

Even though he was tired and slightly inebriated, he led the way into the thick woods silently, moving quickly, as his ancestors had, without disturbing the vegetation. At one point, Debra and Johnny lost him. The eerie quiet frightened Debra, and in her overwrought state she imagined that William was "gone' too, and, as Betty Lou was, he was now a spirit, floating without substance. She felt light-headed and the talk of "evil" convinced her that the gnarled oaks, seeming to weave in the morning haze, were ancient totems dancing a warning.

Suddenly, she couldn't breathe; the humid air made her feel as if she was filling her lungs with water. She grabbed Johnny's arm. When he saw her panic-stricken face, he said calmly, "Easy, now. Take a deep breath and slowly exhale. That's right. Nothing's going to harm you. You're going to be a little scratched, though."

She looked down at her bare legs and realized that her white shirtwaist dress and white flat shoes were not adequate protection. Large welts had formed on her legs where weeds and small branches had cut her. She didn't feel any pain.

"Here's William. Let's hope that wherever he's taking us is nearby," Johnny said quietly.

It was. With a finger to his mouth to indicate silence, he led them to a cluster of trees that overlooked a clear area. They stood in back of the trees and behind some bushes, obscured from view. A large maintenance building was in the clearing. Its windows were blackened and it had a large double door, big enough to allow a tractor or truck inside. The building fronted a dirt road that ran between the trees where the three stood and the building. A camper-type van was parked by the building's entrance.

"Jim's car was here for about an hour this morning, about two a.m., I guess," William whispered. "I came here to do some thinking last night after I heard about the accident on the radio. I haven't been to this north side of the park for over a year. No reason to, really. Your site plan, Miss Debra, shows that there's just going to be nature trails through this section. Well, imagine my surprise when I stumbled onto this here dirt road and saw the building! Then, I saw people coming and going in vans. Something told me to hide. Sure enough, pretty soon Jim Fixx arrives in his big Caddy and goes inside. Then I see him come out carrying some packages and I begin to notice this odor about the place. And I knew what it was. You know that tiny section of Harmony where the black folks live? Lordy, they've lived there since they were freed. Well, I have a lady friend who lives there and she's scared all the time 'cause of the 'crack factory' on her block. Everyone knows about it, the odor gives it away. But white folks don't much care if black folks hurt each other, so no one bothers them. But it's evil, and now we have evil on the land and it involves white folks living off the misery of others."

Debra and Johnny strained to hear William's hoarse whisper and to understand him. That he was agitated was obvious. What to do next wasn't.

The double doors of the building opened suddenly and four people came out carrying packages. Debra immediately recognized Sara, the silent Amazon from Luther's ranch, and the handsome blond man, also a ranch hand. Next to her, William stiffened and drew a hissing breath through clenched teeth.

Silently, the three watched the others load the van. After each of the four made several trips between the van and the building carrying packages, Sara locked the double doors and got behind the driver's wheel of the van. The three young men climbed into the back of the van. Sara then drove from view down the dirt road.

Johnny, Debra and William simultaneously exhaled as if they had been holding their breaths during the procedure. Without saying a word, William turned and retraced his path through the undergrowth. Debra and Johnny followed.

When they arrived back at William's "camp," the three stood quietly, looking at each other.

William spoke first. "I'd swear on my granddaddy's grave that Mister Luther doesn't know."

"Those four are his ranch hands, William, and it's on some of his original land," Johnny said.

"It was his land, but it ain't now. That building is either right on the border between the park site and Jim Fixx's land or all on Jim's land. I've heard the men talking at the ranch. Jim's bought the land north of the park. The sale was to some company out of the States, but the real owner is that little mean fox, Jim."

"How do you explain Luther's ranch hands?" Debra asked.

"Bad apples. I tried to warn Mister Luther that they were taking advantage of him, living on his land, having wild parties, and barely putting in a good day's work, but Mister Luther just said I was getting crotchety in my old age and didn't remember how it was to be young."

William leaned against the tree and wiped his forehead with an old red bandanna. The drinking and the discovery seemed to have aged him. He looked old, weary, and confused. His malformed shoulder was more pronounced than usual.

With deep sorrow he said, "I have to warn Mister Luther. I'll bring him here and show him. Then he and I can burn the place to the ground."

"No, William. Don't do or say anything yet. It could be very dangerous. Promise me you'll wait a few days before telling him, okay? Debra and I will figure out what to do and let you know," Johnny said.

Debra felt her heart contract for the old man. He was strong and proud; all he wanted was to keep his and the land's dignity. Somehow events were robbing him of that simple request.

"Please go home, William, and rest. Listen to Johnny and just let things ride for a few days, will you, please?" Debra pleaded.

"Don't worry about me, Miss Debra. I'll listen to you two young'uns. A couple of days won't make any difference; this damn drug operation's been going on for months, probably. I won't worry Mister Luther about it just yet."

Debra and Johnny left William sitting under the tree. They had his word that he'd go home "real soon."

As they drove from the park site, Debra said, "The whole thing's unreal. First Betty Lou's death and now a crack factory! We have to go to the sheriff."

"There are some things you should know, Debra. Joe Casey wanted to tell you our suspicions last night at the hospital, but I stopped him. After this morning I think you should know what we suspect. Last month, a retired couple living in Hidden Palms, a development about a mile from the park site, told Joe that the private airstrip on the development has a lot of late night activity on it. Frank Marillo and Bobby put that airstrip in three years ago when they developed Hidden Palms. They said they wanted to attract up-scale buyers that owned private planes. Only four of the lots sold in three years. Five months ago, an off-shore investment group called Antilles Development Corporation bought out Frank and Bobby. Then Bobby started talking to Joe about land that he, Jim, Rufus and Stanley were buying around the park and the proposed bypass."

They were driving on the county road back to town and Johnny swerved the car slightly to avoid a dead raccoon.

"Johnny," Debra interjected, "everyone knows that some of the 'boys' are buying that land. They know it'll increase in value when the park's complete," Debra said.

"Right. But only a few small parcels are in their names; the land Bobby described to Joe as 'his' is listed in the county court records as owned by the Antilles Development Corporation. Joe checked. Joe's been watching the 'boys,' as you say, and he suspects they are involved in some land scam through this investment corporation. He also thinks that the corporation is laundering drug-trafficking money from this county. Haven't you ever wondered how Jim Fixx, who owns a small seafood restaurant in Port Pompano in the next county south, can afford to drive a new Cadillac every year? And how about all that gold jewelry he wears?"

"I just assumed he had lousy taste."

Johnny gave a short laugh and continued, "Joe and I have talked at length, Debra, and we're pretty sure that you, some-how, upset an elaborate network of land scams and drug-traf-ficking when you got that state grant. Now you can add drug manufacturing to the list," Johnny said grimly. "Betty Lou's accident may somehow be connected. It seems to me that wherever drugs are, death is."

"So we call the Sheriff's Department, have them stake out the crack factory and catch Jim Fixx," Debra said.

"Do you really think that would bring to light a possible land scam involving the park and the land around it? And would Jim's arrest answer questions about Betty Lou's accident? I don't think so. And here's something else you should know: Jim Fixx's brother-in-law is the sheriff and Frank Marillo's cousin is his first deputy."

"Oh"

"I'm going to say the same thing to you as I did to William: let's just wait a couple of days. I'll figure something out and then we three, four with Joe Casey, will talk. Meanwhile, don't say anything to anyone. Are you seeing that Alistair fellow regularly?"

Johnny's question surprised Debra. Alistair, indeed all personal concerns, seemed to be from another lifetime. She answered with a simple, "Yes."

"Say you're too upset to see him for the next couple of days. He may be involved. I saw him talking to Stanley at a bar after our last planning meeting for the telethon."

Debra looked at Johnny's profile as he drove. Where was that sweet man she found so endearing? In his place was a cynical, and possibly jealous, man.

"He needs investors in the team, Johnny. I told him to talk to those fellows. For heaven's sake, things are bad enough without suspecting that everyone in the county, and even in Tampa, is involved!"

Johnny said, "Suit yourself. Just be careful. I'm going to drive to our ranch and let you borrow this car. I'll use Mother's. Do you need me to help with the funeral arrangements?" Johnny asked in a distant manner.

"No, thank you. I'm sure they contacted her stepbrother in Atlanta. I'll coordinate it with him over the phone. Thank you for the car. I'll return it as soon as I get a leased car," she answered, wondering to herself, *Where's Johnny?*

The phone was ringing as she opened the office door. The answering machine clicked in on the call just as Debra picked up the receiver. Then she heard Betty Lou's recorded voice saying "Hello" and asking the caller to leave a name and number. The surreal moment transfixed Debra. Just before the "beep," she fumbled with the answering machine, turned it off, and identified herself to the caller.

It was Tommy Thompson and he was distraught.

"That was Betty Lou's voice, wasn't it? God, that's weird. I just heard she died this morning. Sorry. Listen, I can't talk right now, but it's very important that I see you right away. Can you meet me at the Palms Bar and Grill on Main Street?" His words were rushed and he spoke without pause.

By the time Debra called the hospital and then the stepbrother, who told her he was flying in that afternoon, over an hour had elapsed. New Harbor's Main Street was deserted under the hot sun; its only inhabitant was a mangy dog that lay panting on the sidewalk as Debra parked the car. The ramshackle bar and grill she entered seemed to lean on the boarded-up dry cleaner's next to it. The transition from the white glare outside to the dank and dark interior of the bar momentarily blinded her. She stood uncertainly near the entrance until a firm hand on her arm startled her.

"We're in the back. Follow me," Tommy whispered.

They walked past empty tables to the booth farthest from the door. It was dimly lit by the light from the nearby kitchen entrance. A young woman sat huddled in the far corner of the booth, her features partially hidden by her long black hair that fell in lank concealing curtains.

Tommy slid into the booth next to the young woman and Debra sat opposite them. Her eyes adjusted to the darkness and she could see that Tommy's face was haggard.

"This is Nancy, Debra. She's frightened about talking to you, but she knows she must. When we heard about Betty Lou, we knew we had to tell you what we know. Go ahead, Nancy, tell Debra what you heard in June."

June? Debra wondered. *What happened almost three months ago to scare this person?*

"I'm Harvey Brown's secretary, ma'am. I was there when he found out about the grant you received for Palmetto Park and I was there when Mr. Bradenburg and he talked about it!"

In halting words, prompted at times by Tommy, she related the conversation as well as she could remember it. Debra's half-formed suspicions were confirmed. Luther and "the boys" never wanted the park project to succeed. It wasn't clear to Debra how Luther's plans tied in with what she and Johnny had learned that morning, but it was obvious that there was an elaborate scheme involving many of the board members, including Jim.

Tommy interrupted her thoughts: "When Nancy told me all this in June, I told her not to get involved. We decided that telling you wouldn't change anything. We thought, 'Well, the men are powerful and will get their way, regardless.' We were sorry for you, and for the end of the park project, but I figured it wasn't worth losing our jobs. But then things happened and Betty Lou was killed and we realized you might be in danger."

Debra noted with a jolt that he said Betty Lou was "killed," not that she "died."

Tommy continued, speaking softly, "Bobby, Frank and Jim are running drugs, Debra. They told me about their operation, and the 'factory' on Jim's land, and asked me to fly Frank's company plane for the 'runs.' Palmetto County is a point on a three-pronged operation: the Caribbean, Palmetto County, and Miami. I think Jim or Bobby somehow caused Betty Lou's 'accident,' thinking it was you in that car. They can't let you involve the state in the park project. It's too close to their drug operations. Anyway, I've quit as Frank Marillo's company pilot, and Nancy is giving her notice to Harvey Brown. We're going to get married and live on my pa's farm in the next county for a while until we decide what to do next. If, or when, the drug running is discovered, I'll probably be implicated. We think you should get out of the county also, Debra."

"Thank you, both of you, for telling me what you know. There's no proof, though, that I'm in danger. Right now I don't know what to do. What I want is a few days to think. I'll call Stanley Zaluski and tell him I'm taking some time off to mourn Betty Lou."

"Please don't tell anyone we talked to you," Nancy whispered.

"No, of course not. You two go to the farm and I'll call you there next week."

"Fine. Here's the number," Tommy said as he handed her a slip of paper. "We're going to leave by the back way through the kitchen. Listen, maybe I'm going through post-Vietnam jitters, but I'm telling you, lady, watch your back."

They left. Debra turned around in the booth and looked over to the entrance and the old battered bar. The only other person in the place was the dim figure of the bartender slowly wiping glasses. She hadn't noticed him when she arrived. She longed for a cold beer but she didn't want to draw the bartender's attention. The best thing for her to do, she knew, was to leave the bar quickly, call Johnny and tell him what she learned without using Tommy's or Nancy's name, and then call Stanley and request time off. Then she planned to sleep for twenty-four hours.

Chapter Fourteen

Luther and Jim sat on the bleachers in the hot sun and sweated. Sitting next to them, shirtless and wearing tennis shorts, Alistair lazily stretched his tanned body. He wanted to receive maximum sun exposure while he watched the team on the practice field.

"Where are those damned drinks anyway? What did your man do? Go to Cuba to get the rum?" Jim snarled.

"Easy, mate. The bottle's in my office. Maybe the coke machine is broken again. I told you we lacked amenities around here. Maybe when your money's invested we'll build a bar, right here in Tampa next to the soccer field, and we'll name it 'Quick Fixx.' How's that?" Alistair answered with his usual good humor.

"Real funny. Listen, if Debra doesn't leave there might be a delay in the 'investment'," Jim responded.

Luther, who was sitting quietly watching the soccer team practice with unfeigned interest, turned to look at Jim.

"Nothing seems to discourage her, Jim. Stanley said she called him Wednesday to request some time off and then told him she'd be back at work next week. Stanley asked me what I thought about the just released newspaper report that stated a

155

man saw a car with Dade County license plates force Betty Lou off the road. What about that, Jim? It keeps going round in my mind for some reason."

"So what are you thinking? What do you want to hear, huh?" Jim said and shrugged his shoulders. He turned his back slightly to Luther and said to Alistair, "Listen, Gorgeous, forget your tan for a minute. Luther, Bobby, and I will get you your money, like we said, but you've got to help us get rid of Debra."

"What do you think I've been doing? I tell her all the time to dump this park obsession. That was the deal I made with you. I'd try to woo her away. Hell, the night of the accident I was reporting to Stanley that I was making progress, but things of that nature can't be rushed. What do you want from me, anyway?"

"More. I want more. You haven't earned that money yet. You've just been fucking around, in more ways than one. Here's the plan: next time you're doing what you tell us you do so well, I want a photographer there. I want Debra in a compromising position and I want it on film. Confronted with exposure, she'll leave."

Luther shifted uneasily on the hard bleacher and said, "Now, now. Isn't that a little extreme? If we play in the mud we'll all get dirty."

"Get with it, old man. It's too late to worry about getting 'dirty.' You're in this up to your Stetson. Whether you know it or not, it's past time to be reluctant," Jim countered, with little regard for Luther's sense of dignity.

Before anything further could be said, the soccer team's "go-fer" arrived with the Cuba Libre drinks.

As soon as he left, the men took satisfying swallows from the tall glasses. Then Alistair, whose outward attention was still on the practice game, said casually, "I'm taking Debra down to Sarasota tomorrow, Saturday, on Bobby's cruiser. Just the two of us for a recuperative, romantic weekend. We'll dock near Marina Jack's. How's that fit in with your plans, mate?"

"Perfectly." Jim answered. "I'll call you this evening about the arrangements."

Luther put his half-finished drink on the bleacher in front of him and rose to leave.

"It's been interesting to see your boys play, Alistair. I'm looking forward to having more than a passing interest in this game. Now I must go. I told Aunt Alice I'd get a book she wants here in Tampa. Something about the early Indians in this area. Also, I told William I'd meet him at six o'clock on the park site. Poor old fellow. Betty Lou's death must have upset him. He kept telling me, over the phone, that there was 'evil' on the land. Said he found something bad not far from his old 'resting place.' Indians can be real strange sometimes."

As Luther turned to go, a burly soccer player clambered up the bleachers to the men.

"Alistair, we need you on the field for a minute," he said.

"Rick, I'd like you to meet Luther Bradenburg and Jim Fixx. You'll be seeing more of them. They're our new investors," Alistair said, smiling.

Chapter Fifteen

Tiny, uninhabited islands dotted the Gulf waters offshore. They seemed to float like green bars of soap in a huge bath of warm water.

Debra was amazed at the brilliant aquamarine color of the water and at its warm temperature. The bathtub analogy frequently occurred to her; the Gulf was usually so calm that hardly a ripple hit the shores. Its shallow, sandy bottom was like smooth, white porcelain and the water temperature hit 86 degrees in the summer.

She and Alistair took the Intracoastal Waterway, the "lazy man's water route," to Sarasota. Staying between the barrier islands and the shore, the cruiser slowly sliced through the water passing clusters of mangroves on the islands. Their tangled, exposed roots reached into the water, providing hideaways for little mammals and look-out places for water birds hunting for the tiny fish that flashed between the roots in the clear water. Debra basked on the upper deck, knowing her emotions were playing havoc with her mental stability even as she appreciated the scenery. She stared into the clear water and imagined sliding off the boat and sinking into the warm liquid womb below. She wanted peace. The "sleep cure" hadn't worked. She still didn't know what to do. And Johnny hadn't been a help. Her fragile alliance with him was, apparently, dissolved. When she finally reached him on Thursday to tell him what "two people" had told her about the land scam and the drug operation, he had been polite, but aloof. He told her to rest and to keep the car over the weekend. She didn't bother to tell him that she wouldn't need it.

Alistair was a comfort to her. After he expressed his sympathy over Betty Lou's death again, he stayed at the cruiser's controls and allowed her to be alone with her thoughts. But her thoughts were becoming jumbled. She had to talk to someone, she realized. She needed to talk, and then she needed someone to tell her what to do. She decided it was time to trust Alistair.

Rushing from the upper deck to Alistair, she put her arms around him from behind, and placed her cheek against his broad back as he stood, Viking-like, at the controls.

"Alistair, I must talk to you or I'll go crazy. Just let me tell you everything that's happened. Please don't interrupt. Just listen and then tell me what you think, okay?"

"Sure, luv. I don't want a crazy first mate, so talk away!"

She gave him a quick squeeze and then sat in a deck chair in back of him.

"I know you're happy to have Bobby as a new friend and as a potential investor, but you have no idea what he's really like. Or what all those 'good ol' boys' are like. Sure, you've told me to leave the project because it's so dreary living up there, but what you don't know is that it's dangerous. Alistair, you and I have been so stupid! So involved with each other and our separate projects that we haven't seen what's been right in front of us for months!"

Then she told him everything: she told him about the crack factory William had shown her and Johnny, and about Bobby's and Jim's drug operation; she told him about Luther and Harvey's conversation regarding the state grant and the intent to sabotage the park project, and she related the growing suspicion that Betty Lou's death wasn't accidental. Ending her monologue, she said, "Joe and Johnny think that the powerful men on the board are involved in some major land scam and are using a Caribbean corporation as a tax dodge and as a purchasing front. Maybe they are all involved in the drug trade and are using the front corporation to launder the money. And Luther's power somehow reaches all the way to Ed Haze, Commissioner of Agriculture."

Alistair slowed the cruiser when she finished talking and took it into a small cove where he dropped anchor before turning to her with his response.

"Luv, you must resign from your job this evening. You must call Stanley at his home from Sarasota and you must resign! You hear me? What you've just told me scares the hell out of me and that takes some doing. Dear lady, you are in deep danger. You are 'up to your armpits in alligators,' as they say around here."

"But aren't you angry, Alistair? Don't you want to expose those 'reptiles' for what they are? They've duped a county-full of nice people, state legislators and stupid, idealistic me! And if, indeed, they killed Betty Lou, who's going to see that they hang for it?"

"Not you. Not me. They'd try to kill you again if you tried."

"They wouldn't risk it. It would be too obvious. No one would believe the accidental demise of both Palmetto Park employees. Besides, they'd have to get rid of Johnny, too. He knows everything I do. And now you know, also."

Alistair didn't say anything, he just held her while the two of them slowly rocked with the soothing motion of the anchored boat as it rode the gentle swells.

Then he said, "You're safe with me. We're going to have a beautiful afternoon and evening, and I'm going to convince you to leave those bastards to their own fate. Just relax and let me take care of you," he stated calmly as he pulled anchor and resumed their journey.

Debra felt some of the tension leave her. It may be counter to feminist philosophy, she thought, but twice recently she had felt secure — once in Johnny's arms on her dock and now in Alistair's.

They docked the cruiser at Marina Jack's, a waterfront restaurant in Sarasota. Alistair, happy to be a tour guide, called a taxi to take them to the Ringling Museum of Art. As they rode there, Debra realized that Sarasota was a world away from the rural Florida she had been immersed in for so many months. It was that tropical, elegant paradise of her imagination that she had sought when she left California. Broad boulevards, lined with tall, graceful palm trees, curved along the waterfront. Pastel colored buildings, faintly Mediterranean in style, contained expensive shops and art galleries. There were flowers everywhere. She saw sparkling white sand beaches; luxury yachts bobbing in the Gulf water, and tanned people driving foreign cars. Her dear departed BMW would have found friends here, she thought with amusement.

For an hour they toured the lovely old museum built with circus money to house John Ringling's collection of baroque art. Debra, for that space of time, left the horrors of Palmetto County behind her. The cool ornate rooms with their high ceilings soothed her. The paintings, many of them depicting religious anguish, helped her to put the turmoil and pain of recent events into a historical perspective. The greed of small minds lost power over her. She realized that she had been living with spiritual and aesthetic deprivation in Palmetto County. She also knew, without saying anything to Alistair about it, that she wasn't afraid anymore or in doubt about what was the right thing to do. She was going to expose those petty, evil men somehow.

The cab ride from the museum and across the causeway to the barrier island, St. Armands Key, was more visual "food" for Debra. Everything sparkled — the homes, the Gulf waters, and the white sand. It all looked so clean. St. Armands Circle, a collection of restaurants and boutiques on the key, reminded her of elegant beach towns in California except for the absence of heavy traffic and pedestrian congestion. The ambiance of the Sarasota area was familiar to Debra. The feeling of familiarity, coupled with Alistair's presence, eased her fears and made her resolve, formulated at the museum, firm.

He took her to a Spanish restaurant he knew on the "Circle," and insisted that she order black bean soup, one of the restaurant's specialties. He also ordered a bottle of wine for them.

"People in Florida, particularly transplanted Cubans, can never agree which restaurant serves the best black bean soup," he said as soon as the waiter left. "This place is my choice. Come on, Debra! Lighten up! I'm making 'small talk.' Forget everything bad, at least for a while. After we eat, you'll call Stanley and resign and then maybe we'll cruise back by starlight and anchor near an island rather than spend the night in the marina."

"No, Alistair. I'm not calling Stanley. I'm not resigning until those men are exposed for what they are. I probably can't save the park project, but I can, with your help, stop them from hurting more people," Debra said quietly.

He didn't respond at first. He looked at her determined face, and then shrugged slightly.

"You don't know what you're saying or what you're letting yourself in for. You have to change your mind."

"No, I won't."

"Well, then, we'll jump into the fray together. But tomorrow we'll decide what to do, not tonight. Tonight, I'm going to get you slightly drunk and ravish you. Deal?" he said, putting out his hand.

"Deal," Debra laughed and shook his hand.

———————

It certainly had been easy to ply her with wine, Debra realized two hours later. She was wonderfully relaxed; not aware of anything except the gorgeous sunset, the tropical ambiance, some random, inconsequential thoughts, and the heady proximity of her handsome lover as she and Alistair sat on the cruiser docked at Marina Jack's. Silently, they watched two plump manatees slowly make their way between the boats tied-up at the restaurant's dock. "They're odd looking," she murmured, "I wonder why they're so lovable?" She felt free of all worries, sensual, and invincible.

Chapter Sixteen

Johnny pushed the accelerator of his mother's old Lincoln Continental to the floor. The car responded sluggishly and he hit the steering wheel with the palm of his hand. It was taking forever to get to the park site.

Where is she, anyway? he wondered as he recalled what had happened at her house earlier and his confrontation with one of her neighbors. Frustrated by calling her at home and getting no response, he had driven there late in the afternoon. His Corvette had been parked in the driveway, locked, and there had been no answer when he rang her doorbell. Johnny had cursed softly. He was worried about Debra, and he was upset that he had left the extra set of his car keys at home. He couldn't exchange cars. Still muttering, he had walked around the house. As he circled it, he had peered into her windows. He had been at her bedroom window when a voice in back of him made him jump and whirl around.

"What do you think you're doing, young fellow?" A tiny, white-haired man was holding a shovel, almost as tall as he was, in one hand.

"I'm looking for Debra Price. I'm a friend and I'm worried about her."

"Friends don't creep around a house peering into a person's bedroom. This is a nice neighborhood. Now get yourself along."

Johnny had suddenly visualized a humorous scene: this little gnome chasing him while brandishing his garden "weapon." He had imagined a vigilante brigade of elderly people hiding in the bushes armed with hoes, rakes, and watering cans.

Suppressing a smile, Johnny had reassured him, "Really, sir, I am a friend of Debra's. Did you see her leave the house?"

"We mind our own business around here, fellow. But it just so happens I was outside getting the newspaper when I saw her leave this morning."

"Someone must have picked her up because the car is still here. Did you see who it was?"

The man, still on the alert, had looked intently at Johnny. Apparently, the boyish face softened him somewhat because he answered, "Can't see that it's any of your concern even if you are a friend. But I'll tell you anyway. I couldn't see the driver but the car was one of those German ones."

"A BMW? A Mercedes?"

"A Kraut car, boy. They all look alike."

Johnny had given up questioning the man and thanked him. The neighbor had followed him as he walked back to his mother's car. When Johnny had driven away, he had glanced in the rear-view mirror. The man was still standing in Debra's driveway, shovel in hand, watching the departure.

Now Johnny was late for his meeting with William at the park site. As he drove he tried to remember who drove a German-made car. Bobby had a Jaguar. Maybe that phony Alistair talked her into seeing him, Johnny speculated. The thought of them together made his stomach knot. The last few days had been miserable for Johnny. His usual easygoing attitude was gone. He regretted his distant manner with

Debra during their last conversation, and he knew it had been caused by fear. He was afraid for her and he didn't know what to do with the dangerous information both of them had. It was unusual for him to be afraid and unsure of himself. He was used to taking action to solve a problem, not with pondering consequences. Instead of telling Debra how he felt, he had been coldly polite to her. Now she had gone someplace without telling him. Johnny was glad to have William to talk to and hoped that a plan of action would result from their meeting. At least he would tell William to keep quiet about the drug operation just a little while longer. Maybe the thing to do was to bypass the local law enforcement fellows who might be tainted and go directly to the federal authorities.

Johnny drove into the park site and saw the sheriff's car parked next to Luther's jeep near one of the dredged lakes. A deputy sheriff's car was off the road closer to the lake. He saw Luther standing at one end of the small lake watching the two lawmen bending over something at the other end. Johnny parked the car and ran to Luther.

The rancher's face was white and his eyes, when he looked at Johnny, were red-rimmed and vague.

"What's happened?" Johnny shouted and grabbed the man's thin arm.

Luther flinched and said, "I found the body a half-hour ago. Just floating there, so peacefully. It didn't register at first. I thought, 'what's that old Indian up to now?' And then I thought, 'why, even wily old William can't swim that long without breathing, face down'."

"William's dead?" Johnny asked incredulously.

"Yup. Dead. Can't believe it myself. What are you doing here?"

Johnny felt a sense of profound loss sweep over him. He answered, "William called me yesterday and said to meet him here at five-thirty today."

"Funny. He was setting up meetings all over the place. I was supposed to meet him here at six o'clock yesterday evening. I was here but William never arrived. I was worried because that's not like him. This morning I went to his trailer, but he wasn't there. Then I started looking around the park site for him. Never occurred to me to look in the lake. Maybe I wouldn't have found him except for that old red bandanna of his. It was floating in the water near his head and caught my eye." Luther's long thin hands were shaking.

The sheriff walked over to the two men. He cleared his throat and said to Luther, "Looks like William was drunk and fell in. You know Indians."

"Hey! Sheriff! Come look at this!" the deputy called. "This doesn't look like a drowning to me! The old guy's head's been bashed in!"

The sheriff left Luther and Johnny and walked back to the body.

"Who else knew about your six o'clock meeting with William?" Johnny asked Luther quickly.

"Let me think. Why, I guess I mentioned it to Jim and Alistair down in Tampa yesterday afternoon. That's right. I was about to leave to go to that bookstore Aunt Alice loves and I said to them that William wanted to meet me here at six to show me something 'bad.'"

"Luther, I think William was killed and I think Debra is in danger."

"Why would anyone kill William? And don't worry about Debra, she's fine. She's having a romantic fling with Alistair on Bobby's cruiser. They're docked near Marina Jack's in Sarasota, so she's real safe."

Johnny didn't respond to the dazed old rancher; he ran to the car and, before the sheriff could stop him, drove out of the park.

Chapter Seventeen

The fiery tropical sunset was over. For an hour afterward the sky retained tinges of pink and mauve, but now it was dark. The city lights twinkled and some of the yachts in the marina emitted soft lights and quiet snatches of conversation.

Debra and Alistair were still on the deck of the cruiser. He was talking softly; she was quiet. Her earlier, mellow mood had left her. Too many days of sadness and fear, with little food or sleep, hadn't mixed well with all the wine. Alistair, however, made sure her glass was never empty.

"I'll keep you safe, luv, and I'll help you with those bastards." he reassured her. "Time to go below, Debra, away from prying eyes. I've been wanting you all day."

He gently helped her out of the deck chair and carefully guided her below.

Bobby had made sure his cruiser was a proper place for his and his friends' seductions. Beyond the galley and small dining area was the separate master suite, dominated by a bed which was reflected in mirrored walls. Debra, weaving, walked eagerly to it. She wanted to sleep.

"Not so fast! Let me undress you slowly. You've always liked that," Alistair said. He unbuttoned her blouse and removed her bra, kissing her nipples as they were exposed. Then he unzipped her slacks and slowly removed them while she sat on the edge of the bed. To remove her silk underpants, he gently pushed her down onto the bed so that she was prone as he slid the garments from her.

"What a beautiful sight. Now just stay like that."

Groggily, Debra responded, "It's not fair. Take off your clothes, too." Then she giggled as he struggled out of his tight white slacks and cotton pullover. When he turned to go into the galley, still wearing his bikini briefs, Debra said, "Hey! You're not down to the essentials yet!"

"I will be soon. Right now I'm going to get us some champagne."

"Nothing for me. I won't be good for anything if I have anything more."

"Nonsense. You're just relaxed. What's a seduction without champagne?"

She watched him walk through the door of the master suite and followed his fluid movements as he went into the galley and uncorked a bottle. She was having a hard time focusing. That, and because he turned his back at the appropriate moment, prevented her from seeing the white powder from a small vial that he deftly emptied into her glass.

He returned to her carrying two glasses, handed her one, and proposed a toast.

"To our success! Come on, drink up!"

After she took a swallow she said, drowsily, "Success in what? In bed? In getting rid of bad men? What, soccer star?"

"Just 'success.' Now I'm going up to take one last look at the moon and make sure everything's secure. Just stay right there like you are. You make a very sexy picture!"

Debra couldn't have moved if she wanted to. By the time he was at the cabin's ladder to go topside she had passed out. She was sprawled on the bed, the champagne from her tipped glass was splashed over her breasts, and her face was a deathly white.

Alistair turned to look at her before ascending the ladder and then went to a side cupboard in the cabin. He took out a small packet of cocaine, a straw and a hand mirror. Very carefully he placed the mirror flat on the bed next to her, spread some powder on it, and put the straw between her lax fingers.

He then went topside and took a flashlight from a gear box. He aimed it at the parking lot near the restaurant and flashed its light three times as Jim had instructed. Then he waited, leaning nonchalantly on the boat railing.

Nothing happened. There was no movement in the parking lot. Just as he was about to signal again, a car raced into the parking lot, stopped, its headlights were extinguished, and a man jumped out. The large man ran down the dock toward Alistair, quickly scanning each boat as he passed it. The sound of his heavy running on the wood planks shattered the quiet night.

When he was three boat slips away, the two men's eyes locked and they simultaneously recognized one another. Without pausing, Johnny raced toward the cruiser, jumped on board, and threw Alistair to the boat's deck, causing the boat to rock from the hard impact. Johnny pinned him to the deck and yelled into his stunned face, "Where the hell is she?"

Neither man saw the short wiry man with the camera when he scrambled on board behind Johnny. Before Alistair could answer Johnny, a bright flash startled the two men.

Alistair, pinned prone by Johnny, yelled in the direction of the flash, "Not me, you bloody ass! She's down below."

Johnny quickly released Alistair and rose to intercept the photographer. Alistair stood, stooped to get the flashlight, and, straightening himself and swinging in the same motion, hit the back of Johnny's head with the metal flashlight.

Johnny crumpled to the deck.

"Hurry!" Alistair commanded the photographer, who, in his haste, almost fell down the ladder into the cabin. A series of bright flashes illuminated the boat's interior as soon as the photographer found his subject.

Johnny was stunned but managed to get to his feet. With an unintelligible roar, he grabbed Alistair in a wrestling hold and flipped him over the side of the boat into the water.

"Shit!" Alistair said loudly as he splashed in the water and then tried to find a way to get back on board.

The photographer, his business completed, jumped off the boat to the dock and hit it at a dead run with Johnny in pursuit. Johnny's muscles didn't help him in the footrace. The small man got to his car and was in it with the doors locked before Johnny reached him. He started the car and put it into reverse gear as Johnny tried to open the door. Johnny pounded on the car's hood in frustration before the photographer backed up the car and drove away.

Alistair clambered aboard the boat just as Johnny, running back, reached it.

"Take her off the boat, if you want. I don't care. The pictures are taken," Alistair said calmly as he shook his wet hair and wiped the water from his eyes.

Johnny didn't answer him. He quickly moved to where Alistair stood, got him in a wrestling hold again, and threw him back overboard.

"Oh, shit," was, again, Alistair's only response.

Johnny rushed down into the cabin. When he found her, Debra looked dead. "Oh, God. Oh, God," he repeated as he fumbled to find her pulse. When he found it, he exhaled in relief. Quickly, he swept the drug paraphernalia to the floor, gathered her clothes that were strewn around the room, put them next to her on the silk bedspread, and then gathered the bedspread around her and her belongings.

He carried her, wrapped in the bedspread, carefully up to the deck. Alistair was again on the boat, dripping and swearing. He backed into the farthest corner of the deck when he saw Johnny emerge from below carrying his limp bundle.

Johnny didn't even look at him. He left the boat with Debra as quickly as possible.

Chapter Eighteen

"Stop your bawling, woman," Joe Casey ordered Martha, who sat in a large, soggy heap on the couch. "Johnny told us that Doc Jenkins checked her out and said she'd be fine. I brought you to this here strategy session to help, not to be damned hysterical."

Johnny's mother, back from her Sunday worship, looked into the living room as she stood in the hallway removing her hat. It was an interesting collection of people she observed. Martha was crying; Nancy was clinging to Tommy; Joe was pacing the floor puffing furiously on his cigarette; Michael was doodling on a note pad, and Johnny was looking down the hallway that led to the bedroom where Debra slept. Johnny's mother sighed and shook her head in sympathy before going into the kitchen. The house had been filled with tension ever since Johnny's arrival last night with the desperately ill Debra.

Once Dr. Jenkins had been roused from sleep, vowed to secrecy, and had examined Debra, Johnny called Joe Casey and told him everything that he and Debra knew. Joe and he decided to hold a meeting of the "good guys" at Johnny's family ranch. Joe, following a hunch that the "two people" Debra had talked to on Thursday were Tommy and Nancy, hunted the couple down at Tommy's farm and convinced them, none too diplomatically, that they'd regret it if they didn't "stand up for what was right." Joe also roused a groggy Martha from her bed that morning because, he said to Johnny, "There's one 'smart cookie' hidden in there, and her heart matches her size."

Michael drove up from Tampa as soon as Johnny called him.

Once the group was gathered, Joe and Johnny alternated in the telling of the various land intrigues and drug operations. Johnny had just finished his recounting of Debra's rescue when Martha had collapsed into tears.

Johnny continued: "I don't know how long Alistair's been involved or why. Probably Jim and the others have offered him money. People in the sports business have known for some time that the Tampa Bay Smashers are having financial problems. I don't think Alistair killed William."

A loud wail issued from Martha, followed by a curt "hush-up" from Joe.

"But I think Jim did, knowing, or suspecting, that William had discovered the crack factory and was going to tell Luther. By the way, I told Debra about William last night after Doc Jenkins left. She was still pretty doped-up. I don't know if she understood me or not. Anyway, Joe and I don't think Luther knows about the drug operation. We think he's just involved in the land scams. We won't ever know, probably, what happened when Jim and William confronted one another, but I'd bet my life that William didn't tell him that Debra and I also know about it. Maybe I am betting my life, and Debra's."

"I told Alistair everything, Johnny. None of us are safe," Debra's soft voice interrupted. Everyone turned, startled, and saw her standing unsteadily in the hallway. She wore his mother's cotton robe which engulfed her and made her look very small and vulnerable. She was pale and shaking and obviously still ill.

"Good morning, everyone. Before anyone says anything, I want you to know that I'm very ashamed and very sorry. I've been a fool and I'm deeply embarrassed."

Martha immediately rose to go to her, but Debra averted her eyes from the group and walked slowly to Johnny, tears streaming down her anguished face. "Oh, Johnny, William's gone, too, isn't he?"

They didn't embrace but looked sadly at each other while they held hands.

Joe coughed and said, "What's done is done. So, Alistair knows everything, huh? Well, Jim and Bobby can't kill us all, unless Bobby-boy decides to take his turkey hunting skills out of the woods and into the community. I'm betting they'll figure we'll be quiet, for several reasons. For starters, we don't have any hard proof. Hell, they could move that drug operation anytime, or burn it down; secondly, they'll think we're intimidated. We're part of the community and the community works as long as the good ol' boys get their way. And, third, those pictures of Debra. Someone is going to show up with them and threaten Debra with exposure if she talks."

Michael, who had been quiet until now, spoke. "There is proof that they intend to develop the park site into a shopping mall. Seems that about eight months ago, Bobby took a shopping mall site development plan to a colleague of mine in Tampa and said he wanted him to do some design work. My friend didn't want the job and didn't think anything more about it until recently when I told him about my work on the Nature Center. We got together for a few drinks last week and he described the location to me. It's our park, guys. My friend remembered that the site plans were signed by Charlie Towns, a Palmetto County land planner. I say that Johnny and I pay a late night visit to Charlie's office and get our proof."

"That's great, Michael, don't get me wrong, but then what? How do we get the plans before the public?" Johnny asked.

Debra was sitting in a chair next to Johnny, using her hands to wipe her tears. She looked startled by a sudden thought and then spoke resolutely, "The telethon! We'll use the telethon. It's a little less than two weeks away. We'll just keep very quiet until then. What I think will happen is this: one of the men will approach me with the pictures. They'll want the telethon to go on as scheduled so that more community funds will be pumped into the project. Then they'll want me to resign at the end of the telethon in front of Senator Grizzard and the public. They'll probably figure that if I do so, Grizzard will halt the state money. They'll all want to be there on the air — Alistair, Luther, Bobby, Stanley, Harvey, Rufus and Jim, smiling and looking good to the community and to the state legislators. Even Ed Haze, Commissioner of Agriculture, will be there. They can then look properly shocked and dismayed when I resign for 'personal reasons.' God! I'm starting to think like those reptiles!" She laughed shakily. "I'll resign, all right. But then, in front of everybody, Michael will show the real site plans instead of his design of the Nature Center as scheduled. Martha, you're in real estate; you can get copies of all the land transactions around the park site from the county courthouse in Harmony. You'll show our 'viewing audience' who's buying land and you'll introduce the Antilles Development Corporation to them."

Tommy jumped up from his chair and said, "And I'll tell the viewers about the drug runs, even if it implicates me! And Nancy, if she's brave enough, will tell everyone what Harvey and Luther said!"

Johnny said firmly, "I'll tell what I heard the deputy say about William's head being bashed in. The sheriff's probably telling folks that William drowned while drunk."

Joe Casey stamped out his cigarette and said, "Those bastards won't know what hit them. What are they going to do, sue us? Hell, I have some dope --- guess I can't use that word anymore --- on Stanley and his shady maneuverings to help the developers that will fry him!" Joe then paused and said somberly, "But what if they try to cancel the telethon? Or don't show up? We've lost our platform."

"They won't cancel it and they will show up, smiling and charming. Believe me. They'll want everything to look normal." Debra said.

Johnny looked concerned and said, "I'm worried about the plan, Debra. Once accusations start flying one of the men is bound to accuse you, on the air, of being a drug addict and a ..."

"Loose woman?" Debra interjected. "I don't care, Johnny. I've decided to leave Palmetto County. Please, let me finish. What I want to do is to present enough suspicions during the telethon that Senator Grizzard will initiate a state investigation. We can't get the 'bad guys' arrested without proof of the murders and of all the collusion, but we can make it damned uncomfortable for them. And we can protect ourselves from harm. Everyone watching will be our witnesses. We'll be invulnerable to future blackmail or even possible killings."

"And the park project?" Martha asked.

"I don't know," Debra answered frankly. "It's probably finished. That restriction is still in the deed, after all, and if the state money is halted because of an investigation, we can't meet the construction deadline. Perhaps the deed will be found to be invalid. Early this morning, even though I was still in a drugged state, I thought of a possible way for the project to survive.

Maybe. Perhaps Joe's retiree group could be made temporary custodians of the organization. There might be a way the state could do that and still give the organization the money. We'll have to count on Senator Grizzard to help us."

Everyone was suddenly quiet, thinking about the telethon and the plans to expose so many powerful men.

Johnny broke the silence. "I wonder which of those scum bags will approach Debra with the pictures."

✽ ✽ ✽

Chapter Nineteen

As long as they stayed in the shade, the heat was bearable. Fortunately, Palmetto County Community College was well landscaped and had winding oak-shaded walkways between the campus buildings. The two men strolled leisurely in their lightweight tropical suits. Still, perspiration, which they occasionally wiped with linen handkerchiefs, slid from both their faces. They would have preferred to be in an air conditioned building. But there were other people in the buildings and the two men needed to be away from potential eavesdroppers.

"Luther 'read' me correctly, Rufus. I was very clear in stating that I believe the college deserves those mineral rights," Harvey said.

"Why does it deserve them, Harvey, old boy? After all, the Bradenburgs already donated this land we're walking on. Why do you think the college, which is really you, as we all know, deserves another gift?"

Harvey, tight-lipped, stopped walking and faced Rufus. His face was even whiter than usual and ugly red splotches, caused by the perspiration and heat, were on the side of his face and on his scalp, visible through his pale hair.

"Quite frankly, 'old boy,' I don't care what you think I or this institution 'deserve.' I've stood by and watched you and Luther and Bobby and Jim and Stanley, even, skim all the cream off this county for yourselves. I have sometimes knowingly colluded with your plans, I admit, but I did so in the hope that our alliance would bring more power and prestige to this college. I know about the plans for the park site and I have some idea of what all of you have done, and are doing, to insure that you make a handsome profit. Since I am part of the conspiracy it is only fair that I receive something."

"Why, that's real 'up-front' talk, Harvey! I'll tell you what, the Bradenburg Trust is willing to donate most of the mineral rights, excluding the mineral rights on the ranch and the park site, to your endowment fund but you have to help us first. We want that little gal, that little thorn in our sides, to resign on the air, during the telethon, and in front of Senator Grizzard."

The men resumed walking and were silent as a female student walked past them.

Rufus, his eyes following the girl's hips as she walked in front of them before disappearing into a nearby building, changed the subject before Harvey responded. "I didn't see your cute little gal secretary today in the office. You scare her off, or did you set her up in some cozy hideaway?"

"Stupid woman, really. Always walking around the office like a scared rabbit. She gave me her notice. Apparently, she and Tommy are getting married. To tell you the truth I barely notice her absence. I'll find someone else," Harvey responded.

"Tommy quit his job as Frank Marillo's pilot, I hear. Kinda funny coincidence. Wonder what they're going to live on, and where. They're 'dead' in Palmetto County. Real stupid of them to bite the hands that have been feeding them."

"You and Luther know I appreciate what the trust has done for the college. If I can do something to convince Debra to leave, I'd be happy to do so," Harvey said sincerely, "as long as we understand each other."

"I'm sure we do. Say, wasn't that something about William, Luther's foreman? Walked around like he was some kind of shaman or something. Got a little too uppity for his own good, if you ask me. Complaining to people about how the board of directors was 'killing trees' and so on. He was just a drunken Indian. The sheriff says he was probably dead drunk when he fell in the water. Now he's just dead."

"Pity. Now how are we going to convince Debra to resign during the telethon? September first is just a little over a week away." Harvey spoke as he wiped the sweat from his brow.

"Here's a bench in the shade. Let's sit for a minute," Rufus said. As soon as they were on the bench, he continued, "Jim has obtained some 'ammunition' that we could use to fire her, but Luther is too squeamish to use it. He says that it might reflect poorly on the board if the public ever found out what our executive director has been doing. Jim, Bobby and I decided that she should be confronted with what we know and then she'll resign on her own accord. That would please Luther. Did you know that she's been sleeping with both our Johnny and that Alistair Lake?"

"No! Really?" Harvey asked with interest.

"Yup. Right now she's staying at Johnny's ranch. She says that she's recovering from Betty Lou's and William's deaths, but what she's really recovering from is a drug overdose."

"No !"

"There's no doubt at all, my friend. That's the proof Jim has. Take a look at these," Rufus said as he handed the photos to Harvey.

"Oh, Lord!" Harvey's eyes widened as he eagerly scanned each of the photos. "She looks like a porno actress. I mean, what I imagine one would look like. You know, that smart exterior, that calm intellect, never fooled me. If you watch how her body moves you can tell she's just like any other promiscuous woman. Where did Jim get these? Are there more?" Harvey asked.

Rufus smiled slightly at Harvey's avid curiosity.

"I didn't ask him. But now that you've seen these, what do you think? Do you think she should resign?"

"Beyond a doubt. She must be confronted with this proof of her wrongdoing. I've dealt with troubled young people before, you know. I can make them see the error of their ways very quickly. I'm sure I can help Luther by convincing her to leave. May I take these photographs?" he asked. When Rufus nodded his approval, Harvey continued, "I hope I won't have to show them to her, but if my stern talk doesn't move her to do the right thing, these will."

"We knew you were just the man to handle this delicate situation because of your experience with young people. I'm sure everyone is going to be real happy when this is all over. Luther and the Bradenburg Trust will be most grateful for your efforts. Now before this heat and those photographs give us old fellows a heart attack, let's go inside."

Chapter Twenty

Mrs. Holmes, during infrequent introspective moments, knew that she had only loved three things in her life: Johnny's late father, Johnny, and cooking for them. She was surprised, therefore, when she found that her nightly prayers now included Debra and that, to everyone's amusement, much of her time during the day was spent devising schemes to make Debra eat the bountiful food that appeared, seemingly effortlessly, from the kitchen.

Debra and she had just completed their ritual sparring over the amount of food Debra had eaten for lunch when the doorbell rang. Mrs. Holmes clucked sympathetically when Debra jumped at the sound. The poor girl had been on edge all morning, she thought, ever since that strange-looking Harvey Brown had telephoned and asked to see her.

"I'll get the door, Mrs. Holmes. The lunch was wonderful, really. Thank you! Here, let me help you with the tray," Debra said as she hurriedly handed the heavy wood tray stacked with partially eaten food to Johnny's mother.

Taking the tray, Mrs. Holmes said, "If you see Johnny before I do, tell him I'm keeping his lunch warm in the kitchen.

Where is that boy, anyway? He was here less than an hour ago. He said he wasn't going into the firm today."

"He's probably just on a quick visit to some construction site. If I see him before you do, I'll tell him about the food."

Mrs. Holmes and Debra were both leaving the living room, Debra to answer the front door and Mrs. Holmes to return to the kitchen, when the telephone rang.

Debra could see confusion on the woman's face, and knew she was wondering how to answer the door, the phone, and carry the tray at the same time. Debra felt guilty that ever since her arrival a week ago she had disrupted this loving household.

"Everything's all right," Debra said quickly. "I'll answer the phone, tell whoever's calling to wait, and then get the door. I know you have things to do."

With a small sigh, Mrs. Holmes left with the tray to go back to her comfortable, orderly kitchen. Debra ran to the telephone next to the living room chair that was now her "office."

It was the producer from the cable station with a question about the telethon. The doorbell rang again as Debra told him, "Hold on, I'll be right back."

Out of breath when she reached the door, she realized that she was still shaky from whatever drug Alistair had given her. Dr. Jenkins, after subjecting her to various tests, told her and Johnny that she was fortunate to be alive. A swift shot of anger made Debra stand straighter and strengthened her resolve to confront the ugliness on the other side of the door. She and Johnny knew this morning, when Harvey called, that she was about to be blackmailed by one of the "scum bags," as Johnny and Joe called them.

"Hello, Harvey. Sorry to keep you waiting. Come in and have a seat. I'll be off the phone in a minute," Debra said cordially as she opened the door, smiled, and led the way into the living room. The back of her neck tingled as she walked in front of the somber, pale man. She knew his strange eyes were on her and she remembered Tommy's warning, "Watch your back, lady."

She settled into her chair and picked up the waiting receiver, keeping a composed and friendly expression on her face. Dirk would have applauded.

Her conversation with the producer was brief, but gave Debra time to adjust to Harvey's presence which, in spite of his light-colored suit and pale skin, seemed to darken the cheerful living room.

After reassuring the producer that the telephone volunteers would be at the studio early on September first to learn how to handle the phone bank, she ended the conversation by saying with a smile, "Talk to you soon again, I know. Now that we've started 'count-down' on the big day, we'll probably be on the phone with questions every hour!"

When she hung up the receiver she wanted to wipe her sweaty palms on her dress but controlled the urge. Harvey mustn't see her nervousness. Leaning back in the chair, she said, pleasantly, "As you can see, your executive director is still at work, even if I'm not in the office. The Holmes are dear people to offer me the comfort of their home. It helps."

"I'm very sorry about Betty Lou, my dear. Everyone on the board understands that you need some time to mourn," Harvey said.

"I'm mourning William, too. No one should ever forget William."

"Of course not. You've had two severe blows. Actually, that's why I'm here: the board of directors feels that you need to think of yourself for a change. The project has consumed you. Why, even before the tragic accidents it was obvious that you were barely holding yourself together emotionally. To put it bluntly, but with real concern for you, the board thinks it would be best for you, and the park project, if you resigned."

"The whole board of directors feels this way? Alice? Johnny? Joe? Martha? They all voted for this action?" she asked.

"The executive committee of the board did, Debra — the same group that had the power to bring you here."

"And now they want me to leave?"

"Yes, for your own good. We have even arranged for you to receive a very handsome sum of money as severance pay. All we ask is that you resign next week, on the air during the telethon, and that you do so gracefully in front of Senator Grizzard."

"As you can see, Harvey, I'm still working. My mourning has not interfered with the ongoing operation of the project. We received the state grant for the Nature Center and we're now going on the air to get the money to complete the park road system. Please thank the executive committee for being so solicitous of my welfare, but tell them I am not resigning," Debra said firmly. She and Johnny had "rehearsed" this scene. She needed to know, after her refusal, how far the group would go to be rid of her. She didn't have long to wait.

"Is Johnny home?" Harvey asked.

"No."

"That's good, because what I'm about to show you, for your own good, you wouldn't want anyone else to see or know about. It will just be between the two of us. I have proof of your instability, my dear. This proof shows, beyond a doubt, that you are no longer fit to be executive director."

Debra had tried to prepare herself for this moment, but she felt a great shame. The shame was mixed with a loathing of the situation and of Harvey. She also knew now how self-loathing felt. Her hands trembled slightly as she took the pictures he handed to her. When she looked at them, the anger she felt wiped away the shame. The poor woman in the pictures had been violated, and drugged almost to the point of death. Debra felt the same rage she experienced when she saw pictures or heard stories of psychological and physical torture in war-torn countries.

She handed the pictures back to Harvey and asked, in a clear voice, "I won't ask where you got these, just...is this blackmail, Harvey?"

"A harsh word, Debra. But, yes, if it's blackmail to use proof of a person's wrongdoing to protect that person and make that person see reason. Unless you resign during the telethon, these photos will be given, anonymously, to the newspaper. This evidence of your moral degradation would hurt not only you, but everyone who has supported you and the park project."

"Blackmail can be quickly effective, can't it? I guess that's why it's been around for such a long time. I'll resign, Harvey, as you wish, on air."

Harvey nodded his head, put the pictures in his pocket, and then patted the pocket.

"These, and the negatives, will be destroyed after the telethon. I'm pleased you saw reason."

"I'm sure you'll understand if I don't see you to the door," she said.

"Quite understandable. Goodbye, Debra."

Debra sat quietly as she watched him leave. When the front door closed after him, she began to shake.

"Debra! You were wonderful!" Johnny exclaimed as he burst from the partially opened door of the hall closet fifteen feet from where Harvey had sat. He was sweating from his long enclosure, and he had a tape recorder in his hand.

"This conversation will be the end of Harvey Brown's career. We'll use it as evidence during the telethon," he said.

He pulled her up from the chair and embraced her. She broke the embrace with a frantic motion and ran to the bathroom. She was in there ten minutes, vomiting.

Chapter Twenty-One

The two plump gray-haired ladies were thoroughly enjoying themselves. Even though it was supposed to be a serious, secret meeting ("Secret! Isn't that exciting?" they exclaimed to one another), they had baked three dozen cookies and now watched with pleasure as the other thirteen members of the group devoured them. The only thing that wasn't absolutely perfect about the evening so far was Joe Casey's chain-smoking. One of the ladies coughed and discreetly moved her chair closer to the open window.

The living room wasn't big enough to handle fifteen men and women comfortably on a hot August night, particularly since Joe and Marge Casey seldom turned on the air conditioner. It was too expensive to use. Their social security and pension checks were carefully budgeted. Their small stucco house was almost identical to the others on the block; only the front porches differed slightly in details. Their interiors contained similarities, also: framed photographs of grandchildren; ashtrays made during senior citizens' art classes; shells gathered on infrequent trips to the beaches south of Palmetto County, and furniture that was a mix of remnants from their lives in the

North and new "tropical" pieces. Flimsy rattan chairs existed incongruously next to heavy, dark, upholstered couches.

The fifteen people in the Caseys' living room that evening were the decision leaders of a five hundred-member retiree organization in Palmetto County, and Joe Casey was their president. With Joe carrying the banner they had made county commissioners, doctors, insurance agents and developers uncomfortable. They didn't always win when they protested against high hospitalization costs or faulty sewer systems or unethical developers, but sometimes they did, and, along the way, they made people recognize the needs and desires of senior citizens.

Joe was at his feisty best that evening. Even the two ladies in the back of the room stopped chatting and listened intently. As Joe paced the narrow clear area in front of his small portable TV, wiping the steam from his thick eyeglasses occasionally and puffing furiously on his cigarette, he told them everything that had happened concerning the Palmetto Park project and Debra. He even, without going into details, told them about her relationship to Alistair and what Alistair and the co-conspirators had done to her. He told them, also, about Harvey Brown's blackmail scheme. Except for occasional gasps from the women and swear words muttered by the men, the room was hushed during his lengthy, vehement recital.

"This is what we're going to do, friends: we're going to crash that telethon and we're going to demand answers from those good ol' boys. We're going to ask them some tough questions and see what happens. They've taken our park donations, friends, and lied to us. They have abused this county for years, hell, generations! Cute little Bobby is following in his daddy's and granddaddy's footsteps. They laugh at us 'old folks' while they squeeze every dollar out of us. By coming here to Florida we retirees have lined their pockets and they have duped us, cheated us, and made fun of us. It isn't just the 'rich against the poor,' although that's part of it, and it isn't just the 'natives against the newcomers,' although that's part of it, too; it's the strong against the so-called weak. It's time to stop the bullies, friends!"

"Joe," a man asked, "what about this Zaluski fellow? He's a relative newcomer to the area like we are. I see him on the street and he's real friendly. Then I see him before the county commissioners representing the lousy developers, pleading their case so that a property will be rezoned for commercial use. What's his story? Why's he involved?"

"Money," Joe answered somberly. "He is an example of a weak, but once good, man gone bad because he thinks he needs more money. I have carefully compiled evidence of all his shady deals. I'm sure you've heard rumors about pay-offs when the county purchased most of the sewer systems from the developers. Well, I have proof, and I'll be in the studio on September first with the evidence. Marge has complained for years about those boxes of papers I keep in the garage. It's all there, and I might just bring every one of those damned boxes." He paused to wipe his eyeglasses and his forehead. "Now, before the telethon I want everyone to have five questions to ask those boys. Each one of you call me in the next two days, and I'll coordinate the questions, got it? We want to throw around enough suspicion of wrongdoing that the state will open an investigation into the land scams, the drug operations, and the Palmetto Park project. I know we've all believed in the project, but we have to face the fact that it may never happen. However, there's a chance that Senator Grizzard may help us keep the park alive."

When he stopped speaking and finally sat down, heavily, on the couch next to his wife, she rose, with difficulty, and faced the gathering.

Marge was a small woman, almost crippled with arthritis. With her, Joe was gentle and tenderly adoring. Those who saw him confront "city hall" found it difficult to reconcile his combative behavior in public with his patient, loving care of his fragile wife.

The room was quiet as she spoke: "Through the years I have seen my husband's heart broken by innumerable battles against injustice, but I have never seen his spirit broken. As the events unfolded in this travesty of decency he has described to you, I watched him become more and more disheartened as he wondered what to do to stop the men before they hurt more people. I've worried about him and wondered how much stamina he had left. Tonight, in his sometimes harsh manner, he's asking you to help. Please do. Don't be afraid. We really can change things for the better. Joe's taught me that."

Then she slowly sat down and patted Joe's hand. This time when he took off his eyeglasses and wiped them, so did several other people in the room.

❋ ❋ ❋

Chapter Twenty-Two

The adrenalin rush hadn't hit her yet. She still had an hour before she had to dress for the telethon. She knew the adrenalin would start pumping as soon as her nerves signaled "showtime."

She sat in her favorite wicker chair in the "Florida room" and looked across the canal to the simple homes like hers with their sloping lawns and scraggly palm trees. She was feeling reflective and trying, without much success, not to feel self-pitying also.

Maybe she shouldn't have insisted on leaving the Holmes' ranch, she thought. But she had missed her familiar surroundings and the sanctuary of her home.

Once Johnny had accepted the fact that she was no longer in danger since striking the bargain with Harvey, he had no argument with which to counter her desire to be alone. Even Mrs. Holmes had to admit that she was looking better and finally eating. Also, Debra thought with a smile, she had been tired of living out of the suitcase Johnny had packed with an odd assortment of her clothing. He had returned so proudly to the ranch after his trip to her home to get "things" for her stay. Mrs. Holmes and she had laughed when they saw the mismatched skirts, blouses, shoes, and even, to their surprise, two cocktail dresses. They had laughed even harder when he told them of his second encounter with the "shovel gnome."

Johnny was special, she knew. But did she love him? For that matter, what were her feelings about anyone? She was thirty-five years old, unmarried, childless, and she "fell in lust" with inappropriate men. Seven months ago she had entered this county as she would have entered a stage set, ready to "make things happen" and then to exit stage left to her "real" life. The only trouble was that she didn't know what her "real" life was anymore.

Well, Debra mused, she had certainly made things happen. Two dear people were dead, she had almost died, and soon she'd enter a television studio and Palmetto County would explode. Maybe from the resultant debris she could salvage something of personal value to take away with her, such as a little wisdom or self-knowledge.

The overhead fan made its swishing sounds as she watched a small lizard, a gecko, crawl across one of the screens. He puffed his throat sac to attract a female and Debra suddenly thought of Bobby. She wondered what he was thinking as he dressed for the telethon, pulling on his fancy cowboy boots. She vividly remembered her first impression of a Southern gentleman as Bobby arrived to "fetch her" at the Holiday Inn. Alistair was "dead" to her; something to be taken out of a mental box at a later time, after he was properly embalmed in the past, to be carefully examined for clues as to what he had been and what she had been with him.

She realized that she had been so entranced by the stereo-types that the men here had represented that she hadn't recog-nized their complexity. Because of her naiveté, they had manip-ulated her. She wondered how many people besides her had mistaken slow Southern drawls as evidence of slow thinking.

She was suddenly very afraid. How could she possibly think that she and her allies could outmaneuver such clever men? Something terrible was going to happen. Debra was trembling as she left the screened porch and went into the air-conditioned house to dress.

———◆———

"Showtime!" the television producer shouted jovially.

"Don't scare me, Bill, we have over an hour still," Debra answered with a smile, using banter to hide her nervousness. She carefully stepped over the video camera cables that lay snakelike across the studio floor as she walked to the staff lounge where the others waited. She could hear the bluegrass band practicing in the next room and automatically thought of their appearance time: six-thirty. The show would start at six o'clock and run until eleven o'clock, prime time on a Saturday night. She had scripted the show weeks ago: there would be local and regional musical groups; pre-taped tours of the park site; a presentation by a local magician, and several other variety acts, all interspersed with her pleas for donations. The producer had the five-hour script, with its precise time allocations, in the control room and would be calling the shots. No one except Debra's "army," as she thought of them, knew that only three and a half hours of the script would be used.

When she entered the staff lounge, her six allies turned to look at her. Under the harsh lights, Martha, Tommy, and Nancy looked pale and frightened. Johnny and Joe looked tense and ready for combat and Michael just looked tense. She felt a fresh pang of fear for all of them. But as she knew it would, the pre-show adrenalin was keeping her in high gear and helping her to concentrate on the details of the next five hours. There was little trace of her earlier introspection which she had dismissed as self-pity. She was operating on the surface now, doing a job. Her eyes briefly softened when she looked at Johnny, but her words to the group were matter-of-fact. Handing them each a script with the time allocations, she went over the schedule.

"During the third hour, Senator Grizzard, Ed Haze, and Luther will arrive. Martha and I will handle brief interviews with them. Then the rest of the 'boys' will arrive with Alistair. They are under the impression that a friendly, on-the-air wine party will be held in the studio and that each will have a chance to be on camera to tell the audience how wonderful the Palmetto Park is and how worthwhile. After they arrive, I will resign on the air, and Michael and Johnny will present the two site plans; by the way, I want to know how you got the real one. Then Martha will describe the land purchases around the park. Joe, you'll lead your group into the studio about that time, okay?"

"We're ready!" he said enthusiastically.

"Tommy, you and Nancy should arrive during this time and give your accounts. Any questions?"

"What if they try to leave the studio?" Tommy asked.

"If they leave, we'll just take turns going before the cameras and telling our stories." Debra answered. Then she turned to Michael and Johnny. "Okay, guys, how <u>did</u> you get the real site plan?"

"You're going to love this, Debra," Michael said. "Charlie Towns wants to sell his office and move into that new office complex Bobby developed. He asked Martha to handle the sale. His office is now on 'lock-box' so that Martha or any of her associates can show it at odd hours and on weekends without having to use an office key. Johnny and I simply got the lock-box key from a 'totally innocent and unsuspecting realtor,' entered the office, found the site plans -- filed under Palmetto Park, if you can believe it -- copied them and put them back."

"I could lose my license over this one," Martha said with exaggerated worry, and then laughed.

"Do you need an easel?" Debra asked; all business again.

"We've brought two," Johnny answered. "One on which to show the park plans and one for the shopping mall plans."

"Great. Now I'm going to talk to the phone bank volunteers and the cameramen. Good luck, everybody!"

Tommy gave her a thumbs-up salute which she returned before opening the door. Johnny moved quickly to the door and turned her toward him. He looked into her eyes with the silent question, *Are you all right?* and received her affirmative answer when she nodded her head and smiled. Then she looked at the group again and left.

She found the volunteers, mostly women from various garden clubs and development associations, eager and excited to be part of a television show, even if it just meant that their families would see them occasionally during camera pans. Each had a note pad to take down the names, phone numbers and addresses of those who called in with pledges. Seeing their eagerness, Debra felt a twinge of sorrow that those pledges would never be collected, not after what was going to happen three and a half hours into the show. She gave them a pep talk and went outside to talk to the four cameramen who were having their last cigarettes before the show.

They greeted her warmly and she knew they were excited to be doing their first telethon. Normally, they handled the local news, stilted talk shows and the Sunday preaching of a Baptist minister. Tonight was going to be something different. Only Debra, in that small group by the studio entrance, knew how different.

"Fellows, I know you have designated spaces. And Martha and I will really try to bring the guests over to each of your areas for their interviews, but I'm asking you to be a little flexible, to move right in if you see something happening. Bill, in the control room, will be calling the shots, but maybe you can try to second-guess him, okay? It may get rather loose and fast in there. Just stay focused on the action and move around with the cameras when necessary, okay?"

"Don't worry, we're ready," one of them answered with a grin, and the rest nodded. Several of the crew made a "thumbs up" gesture.

"Is the studio set covered for sound?" Debra asked.

"Yup. Bonnie and Herb are operating the boom mikes, and individual mikes are placed strategically on the set. All you have to do is pick them up and switch them on."

"Great. We'll party in the lounge in five hours and drink the wine that the guests leave, okay?" Debra asked.

"Sounds good to us!" one of them answered. Then the four extinguished their cigarettes and followed Debra back into the studio.

"Showtime!" Bill, the producer, yelled. This time it was true. Debra took her position in front of camera number one.

———◆———

The three hours passed in a blur for Debra. At one point she realized that the pledges were rolling in and that the telethon was a success. Her on-camera pleas for money were gracious and her updates on the total money pledged were excited. She was performing in the moment, believing in the cause, shutting out what the reality was. She was doing a job that she knew she did well, and her enthusiasm shone through the camera to the viewers.

When Senator Grizzard arrived with Ed Haze, Commissioner of Agriculture, and Luther, the reality of what was about to happen hit her. Before going over to greet them and lead the senator into an interview, she went to the party table stacked with glasses, wine and soft drinks. While the high school band was on camera, and she was hidden from view, she took a sip of wine. Then she decided to finish the glass.

As soon as the band marched off the set, she switched on a hand mike and walked over to greet the senator, Ed Haze, and Luther. Everyone said jovial "hellos"; she then led Senator Grizzard to a camera for his interview. Martha was positioned with Ed Haze and Luther preparing to follow Debra's interview.

"Senator Grizzard, the Palmetto Park project is in your debt. Your help this year enabled us to receive the state money for the Nature Center. Thank you."

"You and the people of Palmetto County did it, Debra. Your enthusiasm was hard to ignore. I plan to be here for the Nature Center ground breaking, and I plan on being here when you break ground for the Cultural Center."

Debra wanted to hug him. Instead she thanked him again and led him into the background while Martha had Luther and Ed Haze on camera. While they talked, Debra saw the "boys" drift onto the set. Bobby had a young woman on his arm and waved greetings to Harvey, Rufus, Stanley and Jim. She noticed that, as she had imagined, he wore his fancy cowboy boots. Alistair was the last to arrive. She felt his presence even before seeing him. As he walked to the table where the wine was, he attracted a group like a magnet attracted metal shavings. Every female employee of the television station surrounded him.

Jim was standing near Senator Grizzard. Briefly, Debra glanced at him and realized with a jolt that he was staring at her. He raised his wineglass to her in a silent toast. She quickly averted her eyes. Her hands were cold when she grabbed the mike that Martha, after her interview, passed to her like the Olympic torch.

Debra walked slowly to one of the cameras. Its red light blinked on and she began her speech.

"Seven months ago this community welcomed me with a party. It's been an unbelievable seven months, filled with triumphs like the state grant, and tragedies like the deaths of Betty Lou, my assistant and friend, and William Bearclaw, our conscience and my friend. In their absence, I dedicate this evening to them. Because some of you welcomed me with a party when I arrived, I am now saying farewell by giving an on-camera party to the community. Circumstances beyond my control force me to resign." Debra sensed stirrings in the studio and heard a few exclamations. "But the show isn't over, Palmetto County! In fact, the rest of this telethon will be even more interesting! Right now, I'd like to introduce Michael Palmer, a fine architect who has donated the design of our new Nature Center and Johnny Holmes, a member of the Palmetto Park Board of Directors, and our very own Olympian."

The men walked into the camera range, each carrying an easel on which the two site plans were pinned. She handed the mike to Johnny and moved off the studio set to a quiet corner. She glanced at Senator Grizzard and saw that he was looking at her inquisitively. Her heart was pounding as she turned to watch Johnny and Michael. Michael explained how he had learned about the existence of the real site plans. Johnny then explained the difference between the plans and a tense quiet fell over the studio. It was shattered by Bobby's yell, "Lies! Damn lies!"

Debra saw that the cameraman nearest Bobby had moved in closer to him.

"Those plans were drawn years ago! Before the park land was donated," Bobby shouted.

Michael said calmly, "The date on the shopping mall plans is last year's."

Debra glanced up to the control room and saw that Bill appeared to be on top of the situation. He had one camera on Bobby, who was being restrained by Jim, and one camera on Johnny and Michael.

Martha moved quickly over to the easels and took the mike from Michael. She gestured to the cameras to move in and then, with a long paper tube in one hand, she explained how the men had bought the land around the park and pointed out, on the large map which she unrolled and held with Johnny's help, exactly where the land was located in relation to the park site and the projected bypass. As she pointed out the bypass route on the map, "all hell broke loose."

Palmetto County's "Gray Panthers" arrived. Joe was in the lead, and, true to his word, he carried a box filled with papers. The entrance of the fifteen retirees was impressive; they crashed through the double doors and walked onto the studio set like an invading army. One of them was wheeling Marge in a wheelchair. She proudly held another box of papers on her lap. The thought crossed Debra's mind that a bugle call would be appropriate.

Martha stopped speaking as the camera she was on turned to focus on the "party crashers." Two of the other cameras were recording the reactions of Jim, Luther, Harvey, Stanley, Rufus, and Alistair, all conveniently together next to the wine table. The fourth camera was near the side entrance and picked up the arrival of Nancy and Tommy.

Then the retirees began to shout questions.

"Tell us about the Antilles Development Corporation, Luther!" Joe yelled.

"Really, old boy, it's simply a convenient place to put some of the Bradenburg money," Luther replied.

"Don't 'old boy' me! Martha here has just shown everyone how much land this ADC group has been buying. How much is it going to be worth when the bypass is in, 'old boy'?" Joe asked.

One of the plump, matronly women in the posse seemed transformed; her feminine plumpness took on the appearance of hefty strength and her soft face was set in stern lines as she pushed to the front of the group and, practically nose-to-nose with Ed Haze, said to him, "Mr. Commissioner, it has come to our attention that you have used your office to knowingly collude with Luther Bradenburg in a secret and illegal agreement regarding the three hundred acres of land we call Palmetto Park. It is our understanding that this collusion is a payback on your part for all the unrecorded campaign contributions Luther Bradenburg has given you to secure your many reelections. What do you say to that?"

"I say that it is slander, and I say you're all crazy," he replied as he tried to disappear behind the senator's bulk.

Senator Grizzard, meanwhile, was intently listening to everything while he again tried to see where Debra was standing. She met his eyes and made a calm "okay" signal with her fingers. She then moved Tommy and Nancy nearer the action. The senator, correctly interpreting her intent to let things happen, shrugged his huge shoulders and stood impassively as the shouting continued.

Joe, seeing Tommy and Nancy, stopped in the middle of another accusation being hurled at Stanley. When he stopped, Stanley shouted, "I'll sue the damn lot of you!"

"I hope you do, Counselor. Then I can present my evidence in a court of law!" Turning to Nancy and Tommy, Joe continued, "Everyone! Listen to what these young folks have to say!"

Nancy, deathly pale, was flanked by Tommy and Debra, each holding one of her hands. Freeing her hands, she pushed her long hair to the back of her ears, and looked resolutely into the camera.

"I used to be Harvey Brown's secretary. Last June, when the state grant was announced, I heard Luther and Harvey say they didn't want the park to get the money. Luther said he had made a deal with the Commissioner to get back the land and that the land was going to be very valuable. Both men wanted the park project to fail and Debra to leave."

Harvey shouted, "Don't believe her! She tried to entice me and I refused her advances. This is her way to get back at me!"

Luther yelled, "Shut up, you fool!"

Joe yelled at Tommy, "Tell about the drug operation!"

Tommy squared his shoulders and, taking hold of Nancy's hand again, faced the camera as he related his knowledge of Jim and Bobby's drug dealings.

Jim, Harvey, Bobby and Luther all tried to leave simultaneously, but were halted by the gray-haired blockade that had linked arms and stood before the studio's double doors.

Video cameras were frantically moving to cover the action. A video cable tripped both Bobby and Jim as, frustrated in their attempt to leave, they charged Tommy. Just before reaching him they fell on top of each other and then scrambled up from the floor shouting obscenities.

Alistair began to slowly walk over to the side entrance. Johnny saw his attempt and quickly moved to him and locked him in a wrestling hold. Alistair said, with a slight smile, "This is getting to be a bit repetitious, mate."

The boom mike almost hit Johnny's head when, while still holding Alistair, he began shouting the story of Alistair's drug overdose of Debra. Debra pushed one of the cameramen over to them. As she did so, she glanced up at Bill in the control room. He looked like a madman; his hair was on end because he kept running his fingers through it, and his face was flushed scarlet. In the confusion someone had turned on the floor mike that was used to communicate between the control room and the set. Bill's hysterical voice boomed throughout the studio, "What the <u>fuck</u> is going on down there?"

His words reverberated throughout the studio set and momentarily silenced everyone. Then Johnny, still holding a resigned-looking Alistair, continued his account of Debra's brush with death and Harvey's blackmail attempt. When he finished with, "… and I have it all on tape," Harvey, practically unrecognizable in his crazed state, lunged at Johnny. With one hand, Johnny, releasing Alistair, sent Harvey reeling into the wine table.

Over the crash of the overturned table, Senator Grizzard shouted, "Debra! Call the Sheriff's Department." Then, planting his massive bulk in the middle of the studio, he boomed, "No one leaves this place until the law arrives!"

Tommy and Michael blocked the side entrance and Johnny moved quickly to stand next to Joe and the retirees by the double doors. Debra ran to the phone bank on the set to use the one outgoing line. It was the first time since the fracas began that she was aware of the ladies on the telephones. What she saw was high comedy: two of the twenty women looked as though they had passed out over their telephones. The rest of them were frantically answering the calls that lit up the phone bank.

Just as Debra approached the phone bank, a previously sedate woman, who was renowned for her sweet, quiet charm, yanked her telephone line from the bank, and, waving the ripped-out receiver over her head, screamed, "I can't take this anymore!"

Debra ignored her, raced to the outgoing telephone, and called the county's emergency number. Then, her call completed, she ran back into the fray, deftly jumping the cable lines that were moving across the floor. She was reminded of her jumping-rope days when she was a child.

Accusations and counteraccusations filled the studio. Joe and his retirees, arms still linked, were shouting questions at the men huddled by the overturned wine table.

Debra, again pushing a cameraman along with her, approached Johnny and Joe. Just as the cameraman was positioned near the two men, Debra heard Johnny's voice ring out, "You are filthy scum, Jim, and you'll pay!"

Jim rushed to Johnny, oblivious of the video camera and the boom mike that followed him.

"You watch who you call scum, muscle-brain, or I'll hire someone to get rid of you or do it myself, just like I did to that fucking Indian!"

Debra gasped. Joe and the others standing near Johnny and Jim fell silent. Jim, whirling around, saw the video camera five feet from him and the boom mike practically on top of his head. His face, which had been flushed, suddenly went white and he lunged at the video camera, knocking its operator to the studio floor before falling on top of him. He scrambled to his feet, as did the cameraman, just as the sheriff and three deputies pushed their way through the double doors and past the barricade of retirees.

Senator Grizzard shouted to them, "Arrest that man!" while dramatically pointing at Jim. "I do believe he just confessed to murder."

The sheriff hesitated briefly and then looked his brother-in-law, Jim, in the face. He shook his head at the little man and then handcuffed him.

The video cameras caught it all.

Senator Grizzard shouted to one of the cameramen, "Boy, aim that thing at me! I want to talk to the good citizens of Palmetto County!"

Two cameras stayed on the in-studio crowd to get reaction shots and two cameras moved into position to cover the senator.

"Friends, what happened here tonight is what you might call freewheeling democracy in action. From what I've gathered, watching and listening to this here brouhaha, a few people decided to be brave and stood up to some bullies. Whether they did the right thing or not, and whether they have a case against some of these men, is up to a state investigative commission to decide. I'm going to call certain people in Tallahassee and I'm going to demand just such an investigation. One thing I do know is that the employees of the Palmetto Park and some of the members of its board of directors have acted in good faith with you, the citizens of this county. They believe in this project. They have asked for your support, and your legislators' support, in all sincerity. I'm asking you this evening to reserve your judgment, shocked as you may be by the goings-on here, until all the facts are in. But I happen to believe this project shouldn't be abandoned just because a few 'worms got into the apple.' Now where's that gal that put on this show?" he bellowed.

Debra was pushed forward by Martha. As she walked toward the senator, she automatically looked at the studio clock. *Why that shrewd old codger*, she thought, *he's timing it perfectly for a grand finale.*

The clock showed that they had three minutes of air time left.

When she reached the senator's side, he threw a massive arm around her shoulders and drew her closer to his side. She was dwarfed by his bulk.

"Debra, I want to know one thing. While we were on the air 'live,' was this show also videotaped for posterity, or more importantly, any court cases that might be a result of tonight?"

"Yes, sir, you'll be receiving a copy tonight and another copy will be safely locked away."

"You hear that, folks?" he said into the camera. "Why, shoot, as soon as the dust settles on this here hullabaloo, we may all be able to go to our local video store and rent a copy! I think it might be a real popular item! Congratulations, Miss Debra Price! You've just produced the most interesting telethon in television history! Now say 'good night' to the good folks."

"Good night, good folks," she said, and the red light on the camera went out.

Dazed, Debra was hugged by the senator who then walked to where Commissioner Ed Haze stood. Loud words were exchanged, mostly the senator's. Then he went to the control room to receive his copy of the videotape.

She looked around the shambles in the studio. The sheriff was leading Jim, still handcuffed, to the double doors. Two of the deputies were taking statements from everybody and then letting many of them leave. The retirees were already gone, as were most of the "bad guys" except for Harvey and Alistair who were still being questioned by one deputy. Both men were demanding to see their lawyers before answering any more questions pertaining to attempted blackmail and attempted murder. Neither of them looked at Debra as she passed them in search of Johnny.

Debra saw the young woman who had arrived with Bobby. She sat huddled in a corner on the floor with a wine bottle next to her. She didn't look as if she minded being forgotten in the melee. Debra walked quickly past her on the way to the staff lounge, hoping Johnny was there.

The four cameramen still stood by their cameras; they appeared numb from exhaustion and slightly "shell-shocked." One by one, they left their posts and went to the staff lounge. They passed Johnny who was anxiously searching for Debra. He was frantic with worry. He knew she had been subjected to tremendous stress over the last months, and he was concerned that the night's dramatic events and violent confrontations might have harmed her further.

He found her in the staff lounge with the four cameramen, the producer, and the two boom microphone operators. They were sprawled on the old couch and on the floor, laughing. Some of them held half-empty wine bottles. A cameraman held Debra while, her face buried in his shirt, her body shook convulsively. Johnny rushed to her, pulled her to her feet, and embraced her.

When she looked up at him he was shocked. She was laughing uncontrollably while tears of mirth streamed down her cheeks.

"Oh, Johnny! It was the funniest evening of my entire life! I've never had so much fun!"

Bonnie, one of the boom operators, shrieked, "Did you see that lady at the phone bank flip out?"

Debra held on to Johnny as she almost collapsed with renewed laughter.

One of the cameramen, gasping for breath, said, "How about Bill's 'voice from heaven' booming down into the studio?"

Everyone was holding their sides, weak with laughter. Johnny just stood there, dumbfounded. He didn't think he'd ever understand show people.

Chapter Twenty-Three

Some of the musical notes quivered slightly as the tune drifted among the oak trees in William's favorite place in the park. The hands that held the harmonica were palsied, but the player's back was straight. The retiree had the honor of playing "Amazing Grace," Williams' favorite hymn, at the memorial service.

Alice Bradenburg, wearing a long white robe, a large cross on a heavy chain, and several elaborate necklaces of Indian origin, swayed to the plaintive music. When she started to slowly dance around the grove of ancient live oaks, Debra was worried that the lovely old woman would trip over the gnarled roots or become entangled in the flowing robe.

Everyone gathered for William's and Betty Lou's memorial service watched Alice anxiously as she, with closed eyes, moved slowly around the small natural amphitheatre encircled by the stately trees. There was a collective sigh of relief when the harmonica music ended and the old woman sat on the ground. Debra's relief, however, soon turned to suppressed mirth as Alice picked up an Indian drum and began to tap out a ponderous message to the "spirits."

Debra had attended several funerals in the past and had always worried that her nervousness would cause inappropriate behavior, either copious weeping or unrestrained laughter. This memorial service heightened those mood swings in her. She began to bite the insides of her cheeks, which were wet with tears, to refrain from giggling as she looked over the gathering to see if the other attendees were experiencing a similar reaction.

Joe, his wife, and the other retirees that had formed the citizens' posse at the telethon ten days ago, all appeared properly serious. Some of them had brought small collapsible chairs and were sitting sedately with their hands folded. Martha's face was obscured by the shadow cast from the largest black straw hat Debra had ever seen. Tommy and Nancy were standing near Martha, holding hands; Debra briefly wondered if they now conducted all their daily activities joined. They appeared solemn. Unfortunately, Debra glanced at Michael and Johnny, both leaning on a large tree near her, just as Alice, still beating the drum, began to chant Indian incantations intermixed with fervent Baptist prayers. Michael suddenly turned his back to the spectacle and gazed with intense interest at a squirrel scampering in the tree overhead. His shoulders were heaving with quiet laughter. Johnny, on the other hand, appeared to experience a sudden stomachache as he bent double, holding his hands over his stomach. That's all Debra needed. Gasping, strangled laughter escaped from her, which she tried to turn into a loud sob. Several of the retirees looked at her sympathetically.

The chants and prayers ended and Alice slowly rose to her feet. Debra, taking deep breaths to calm herself, noticed that a shadow swiftly passed over Alice and that the luminescence of her white robe was momentarily dimmed. The shadow was caused by the enormous wingspan of a great blue heron as it flew over the small clearing and landed gracefully ten feet from

Alice. It stood calmly as she picked up a metal box, opened it, and began to scatter William's ashes under the oak trees.

Debra began to cry again. She missed William, and she wished that Betty Lou's stepbrother hadn't shipped her body to Atlanta. Betty Lou didn't know anyone there.

The heron stood quietly until the last of the ashes were dispensed. Then, as Alice slowly turned to it and raised her arms, it unfolded its wings and flew skyward. The steady flapping sound it made blended with the sound of a car coming down the newly paved road toward the clearing. Debra watched the heron as it circled high above before landing in one of William's oak trees.

Debra knew, even before seeing the Jeep, that it was Luther, making a belated appearance. She walked over to Johnny and took his hand. "Let's go to where William led us that day," she said.

They left the others and walked into the thick jungle of palmettos, cabbage palms and large ferns. Johnny walked ahead and carefully held the low palmetto fronds back as Debra followed him. They stopped when they reached the trees and bushes that had hidden them on that startling morning. Even though they knew what to expect when they looked at where the maintenance building had once stood, the sight was still a shock. The building had burned to the ground the night of the telethon. No one knew who had done it, but suspicion centered on Luther's ranch hands that had disappeared that evening. Only charred ruins of the building were left.

Four snowy egrets perched on its blackened remnants and presented a visually striking contrast to the debris.

"The Sheriff's Department found no evidence of drugs or drug manufacturing," Johnny stated quietly to Debra. "But, eventually, everything will 'come out.' The investigation of the two 'accidental' deaths won't be dropped; too many people heard Jim's confession and too many people were involved in the drug operation. Someone will talk. We have to believe that there won't be a cover-up; Jim will be found guilty and Bobby will be implicated."

"Senator Grizzard called me this morning," Debra said. "He told me that the state attorney general has officially begun the investigation into all the various intrigues, scams, and crimes committed in this county." Debra lowered her voice to mimic the senator's, 'We have those boys by their balls and they're feeling mighty uncomfortable.' I wonder about that, Johnny. I don't think discomfort is going to make them relinquish their power. They've built a way of life around it. Anyway, Joe's group has been given temporary control of the park project while its nonprofit status and its deed with the Department of Agriculture are being examined. The senator seemed to think there's a chance the project can be salvaged and eventually be given the state money."

Johnny shifted uneasily and stooped to pick a small wild-flower. He handed it to Debra before speaking.

"We've hardly talked since the telethon. What are you thinking through all of this?"

They were leaning, with their bodies touching, on the trunk of the largest oak in the group of trees. Debra didn't look at Johnny as she ran her fingers lightly over the rough bark. When she answered him she spoke slowly.

"I think William would have enjoyed his memorial. And I think the bizarre ceremony was the perfect ending for my stay in Palmetto County. It made me laugh and weep," she paused, and then continued, "I'm going to spend some time with my parents in Michigan, Johnny. I miss them. Then I'm going to call some people I know in arts education and ask what jobs are available in the Los Angeles area. I have friends there wonder-ing what's happened to me. I'll move back. In a few months maybe I'll wonder what's happening to the park project, but maybe I won't."

"You could make this county your home. You could marry me."

She put her hand on his arm and looked into his kind eyes.

"Johnny, you once said that you wouldn't mention your feelings about me, or what our relationship might mean, until I told you I was ready to think about us. I'm not ready. Right now I'm not capable of making any decisions concerning my emotions. But, Johnny, I'm sure I don't want to live in Palmetto County, and, as hard as I try, I can't visualize you in Los Angeles."

"Don't be so sure. One day you're going to look up from your glass of white wine, or your concert program, or your luncheon salad at some Beverly Hills' restaurant and there I'll be…looking out of place and very much in love."

She smiled and felt her heartbeat quicken. Debra knew, at that moment, that she loved him and that she wanted him in her future. She also knew that a little time had to lapse before she was ready. Without saying anything, she moved into his arms and then whispered, "I'll be watching for you." She broke the embrace and led the way back to William's trees. This time, it was she that held back the palmetto fronds as she passed through them so that they wouldn't snap back as he followed her.

Luther was waiting for them in his Jeep. Everyone else was gone. The encircling grove of trees cast deep shadows over the once sunny clearing.

He got out of the Jeep and walked hesitantly over to them. His tall, thin frame seemed frail, and his eyes, when he tipped his Stetson farther back on his head, were sad and questioning.

"You don't believe I had anything to do with those deaths, do you, Debra? You don't think I knew about all that drug stuff, do you?" Before she could answer, he said, "I never thought that things would get so out-of-hand. I thought that the fellows and I would make a little extra money and no one would be hurt. Hell, I even thought the plan was fun; I got a kick from being clever and pulling all the strings. I was a stupid ass, and I apologize." He took off his hat and bowed to her.

Debra saw the bald spot on his bent head and thought how vulnerable it looked. The man was old, she realized; he didn't have many years to live.

"I understand, Luther. I'm leaving Palmetto County and I'll take your apology with me."

He straightened and looked at his hat as he turned it slowly in his hands. "There's nothing I can do for Betty Lou now except to feel real sorry, and there's nothing I can do for William except miss him for the rest of my life and finally know him for the good friend he was. But I can do something for you. I may be bankrupt morally, but I still have the means to give you a parting gift; something to help you settle into a new life."

Debra pointed down the road to the mounds of fill that obscured the site of the Nature Center.

"See that? My contract is still valid so I'll have my severance pay, but I do want a 'parting gift' from you. Get rid of that fill that's smothering the trees over there. There's been too much killing already. Do it for William, okay?"

Luther didn't say anything; he nodded, put on his cowboy hat, climbed stiffly into the Jeep, and left them.

The sound of the receding car combined with another sound. She heard the flapping wings of the great blue heron as it flew away.

About the Author

Since receiving her M.A. in Communication, Blythe Rainey-Cuyler has served as executive director of arts organizations throughout the United States. She has written numerous articles about her performing arts management work. She is the marketing director for Bloomwell, an online legal document service with a focus on families. Blythe lives in San Francisco. Because of her performing arts background, she is a film, music, and theater enthusiast. You may reach her at blytheraineycuyler@yahoo.com.